CALLING *her* BLUFF

A WHAT HAPPENS IN VEGAS STORY

KAIA DANIELLE

Entangled Publishing, LLC
2614 South Timberline Road
Suite 109
Fort Collins, CO 80525
Visit our website at www.entangledpublishing.com.

Lovestruck is an imprint of Entangled Publishing, LLC.

Edited by Vanessa Mitchell
Cover design by Heather Howland
Cover art from Shutterstock

Manufactured in the United States of America

First Edition November 2015

For Nathasha

Chapter One

For a Las Vegas dive, The Sanctuary was pretty quiet. A basketball game was playing on the flat-screen TV behind the bar. The knock of a cue stick breaking the ball formation on the billiards table echoed the start of another game of pool. A muted hum of conversation carried from the few patrons frequenting this joint. But there was no ringing from any slot machines. No rustle of shuffling cards. No roar of bets being called across a crowded craps table. Since this place might be the only spot in Sin City that had no form of gambling in it (thank goodness), it was a popular after-work spot for locals who worked on the Strip.

What this bar *did* have, however, was maybe the most gorgeous man Kamaria Wilson had ever seen. Only three barstools separated them. She shook her head before doing a double take. She could take him home, ride him until the sun came up and then send him on his way. Too bad she didn't have the nerve.

She stuck her hand inside her jacket pocket and fingered her lucky poker chip. *Behave yourself, girl.*

Kamaria held up her shot glass, giving a toast to the man's sinfully good looks, that alluring combination of thick black hair, trim beard, and smooth, sun-kissed olive skin that indicated he spent a lot of time outside. But, her cell phone rang before she could take a gulp. She swiped the screen to make the call go to her voicemail. She was *not* in the mood to talk to anyone. What she wanted was a moment of peace.

She held up the shot again. Her cell phone rang. Again. Kamaria sucked her teeth. Her damn agent could be so annoying sometimes.

She swiped the the phone's screen to answer it. "What?"

"Is that how you answer your phone? If I didn't know any better, I'd think you were raised by vagrants."

"What is it, Chastity? I'm busy."

"Well, I know you're not busy writing because I've been banging on the door to your suite for the last five minutes and you haven't answered."

"That's because I'm not there." Kamaria took a small sip of the tequila. Taking the entire shot while dealing with Chastity would be a waste of alcohol. She hadn't eaten since first thing that morning, so a sip should be enough to take the edge off. Maybe even enough to kill the urge that had been gnawing at her gut since she arrived in town.

There was a good ten seconds of silence before Chastity said, "I thought we agreed that you were going to steer clear of the casinos while you're here."

She huffed a long, dramatic sigh into the phone. "I am not in a casino, Chastity. I'm in a bar. Not getting drunk because I'm talking to you."

"You're at the bar? Great, I'm coming down to meet you."

"I'm not at the bar in the hotel."

"Why not?"

She really wasn't in the mood for playing fifty-seven questions. She flicked a glance at the hottie again. He'd shifted so he faced her. Dark brown eyes. Her fingers ached to play in his tousled, wavy hair. Damn. He even nodded in her direction. She quickly looked away. She almost schoolgirl giggled from his acknowledgment. Nope, not that one. He looked too much like the cover model on her last book. She didn't want to think about books tonight. She didn't want to think about anything.

"Where are you?" Chastity pressed.

She could tell her agent was two breaths away from going off. Good. That's what she deserved for killing her vibe before it got started. This call wouldn't be happening right now if she had just gone down to the casino like she really wanted to do. She wouldn't be feeling like a loser anymore. She'd be winning. *No*. She took a deep breath. She didn't gamble. Not since… "You did have a reason for calling me, right?"

Chastity squeed. The woman actually squealed the word "squee" in her ear. If Chastity wasn't such a kick-ass agent, she would totally fire her.

In an effort to cut off that high-pitched shriek, she said, "Tell me already!"

"Are you sitting down? You need to be sitting down. I just got a call that will blow your mind."

"What call?" Kamaria's tone was now as dry as the desert air outside. She gestured at the bartender for another drink. Drinks were cheap here, so she could afford a couple more, if she kept to the well brands. She didn't have enough money left in her pocket to cover the good stuff. She'd purposely come out without a lot of cash, and she'd left her credit cards and bank cards in the hotel safe. Like a smoker tossing their last pack of cigarettes, she knew to remove the temptation.

Chastity, meanwhile, had been yammering on about something. Kamaria only caught the tail end of what she had been saying, but the words "your book just hit the list" were enough to make Kamaria stop fingering the ten dollar bill in her pocket. "What list?"

"*The* list. *That* list. As of next week, you're a New York Times bestselling author!"

A way too sober Kamaria nearly slid off her barstool. A warmth spread through her chest. Her body felt light like she had been dealt a full house with high stakes on the table. She had gambled everything on making this writing thing work. And now, she'd won. "No way."

Chastity squealed again. "Girl, you did it. You have this industry by the horns! Find a man. Have a drink. I give you permission to take a night off from writing and have fun for once. You deserve it."

"Great. Thanks. Bye." She numbly disconnected the call and stared at the now blacked-out phone screen. What the —?

She'd started writing romance novels more for herself than to gain any type of celebrity. The fact that enough people had gone to the trouble to buy her book to put her on anybody's bestseller list? That shit blew her mind.

"Are you okay?" She was so caught up in her thoughts the unexpected male voice made her jump.

She spun on the stool into a wall of T-shirt chiseled chest. She craned her neck up. And up. Hot guy's eyebrows held a gentle wrinkle between them. His mouth puckered with concern. She could totally suck that pout off his face. If she did, that would be the most perfect "cute meet" ever. She needed to remember this moment for her next book.

And speaking of books, this guy had "hero" written all over him. The alpha kind. A real take-me-to-bed-and-make-me-scream-your-name guy. She squirmed on the barstool. Her girl parts tingled from just looking at him.

No. Nuh-uh. She crossed her legs to curb his effect on her. She was so not going there. Chastity might suggest finding a man, but all she needed were her two shots of tequila. Okay, maybe three. Then she would call the hotel shuttle to take her back to the Masquerade and finish a chapter in her overdue manuscript. That was the plan. A good, responsible plan of which the new and improved Kamaria approved. She glanced down at her phone again, wondering if her overworked mind imagined the entire call. Her, a bestseller? Shock set in. What the—

"Are you okay?" he repeated more slowly. He gently placed his warm hand on her back. Damn, this man was fine. The dark and brooding variety of fine. He tilted his head. "You're staring at the blank screen on your phone mumbling 'what the fuck' over and over."

Oh. Wow. So much for an inner dialogue.

"Yeah," she mumbled. "I'm okay." She directed her attention back to his chest. Because the maroon shirt he was wearing was ugly as hell. But the cotton fabric molded to his muscles. His very large and firm-looking muscles. Even his nipples had perked up to say hi. Dear Lord, every inch of this man was beautiful. She could see herself getting caught up with a guy like this. Which was why she should push him away. "I'm also completely screwed up."

He tensed for a moment then gave a barely perceptible shrug. "Do you want to talk about it?" His persistence was a total turn-on.

No, I don't want to talk about it, Kamaria thought to herself, *I want to go back to the casino and gamble.* She picked up her second shot of tequila and knocked it back. This plan to have a casual drink alone in a safe space was not working. Normal people had drinks in a bar to blow off stress all the time. Why couldn't she? Damn Chastity and her squeaky, good news call. Another unnecessary plot twist in the story of her life. She chewed her bottom lip. She needed a plan B.

"No. I want to celebrate. How about I get completely shit-faced drunk and then go home with you for a nightcap?"

Hot guy took a step back. He frowned, but she didn't miss

the flare of desire in his eyes. "I'm not a one-night-stand kind of guy."

"Good, 'cause neither am I." Her mouth curved into a smug smile. He seemed to be the nice guy type. She made a point of staying away from them. Her cards were on the table now. She bet her saucy response would make a nice guy like him fold. That whole nightcap line should send him running.

"You're trying to push me away—"

Well shit, she hadn't expected him to be nice *and* perceptive.

"But…" The guy removed his hand from her back and placed it firmly on her shoulder. "I suspect you'd rather have someone ride with you than lie with you tonight."

He called her bluff. How unexpected—and intriguing.

He held out his hand. "My name is Jack. How about we talk first? Make sure I'm not a jerk. And then we'll see about me taking you home."

Kamaria had made a living out of being able to read people. His facial expression hid nothing. The only vibe coming off of him was one of genuine concern. It was official. She liked him.

Still, she wanted to see his desire flare again. She touched her lucky poker chip again. It was time to raise the stakes.

She tapped the seat next to her as an invitation to sit. Then, she pointed two fingers at the bartender, indicating to slide another two shots her way. "Fair enough. I'm buying this round."

He hesitated for a moment, then settled his big body beside her.

Bingo. And the lady wins again.

THE NEXT MORNING…

Kamaria stumbled into the Masquerade lobby the same instant that someone won big on the slot machines. Alarms clanged and lights flashed like Liberace come back to life. Chastity's cheers had been annoying, but the woman at that winning slot machine squealed at a pitch that should only be heard by dogs. Kamaria wanted to punch her in the throat. The desert sky outside had lingering purple streaks of night. How did people have that kind of energy at what the hell o' clock in the morning?

She wasn't exactly hungover. Disoriented was a better word. While her eyeballs still pulsed within their sockets, the monkey was no longer on her back. A small victory. But another victory nonetheless. Each of her steps dragged, but her shoulders felt light for the first time since she had arrived in Las Vegas.

She pushed the button on the elevator then leaned against the wall. That's when someone started slowly clapping directly in her ear.

Kamaria jumped straight up. "What in the…"

"If you tell me where you were all night, then I won't post your walk of shame on YouTube."

What, did the woman have her phone tracked? "Screw you, Chastity."

"Ahh, the prodigal zombie girl speaks." Chastity shoved her smartphone back into her bra. That afterglow from her amazing night…yeah, it was evaporating by the minute thanks to her agent's intrusion. Chastity slapped her on the shoulder. The petite brunette's mahogany face had a glisten that only an early morning workout could produce. Her black spandex yoga pants showing off her curves confirmed it. Friggin' morning people.

Chastity pushed a stray lock out of Kamaria's face. "Honestly, hon, where were you last night? Did you gamble?"

Given her past, she deserved Chastity's interrogation, but

the accusation hurt. She raised her chin and fished her lucky poker chip out of her pocket. "This is the last chip I ever won. I haven't played poker in three years, four months, eight days and *still* counting."

But she also hadn't been in Vegas or anywhere near a casino in the same amount of time either. Who was she kidding? It was only a matter of time.

"Then explain why you're dragging in here at five a.m., with your clothes all twisted around your body…" Chastity reached up and pulled the hood of her jacket out from under her collar. "…And your hair looking like that. You do know that one of your dreadlocks is sticking straight up, right? And don't try and bullshit me about being awake because of the time difference—that's why *I'm* up."

Her hand flew up to her hair. Her locks felt like a total disaster, despite her attempts to pull them into a ponytail earlier. She would not let Chastity make her feel bad. She hadn't done anything wrong. "I only did what you told me to do. I had a drink. Correction, *drinks.* I found a man. I celebrated. I'm a New York Times bestselling author. Woo-hoo!" She did a little hop, threw in a whirly thing with her finger—and promptly stumbled as she landed. Uh, she shouldn't have done that. Her head spun from the movement.

Luckily, the elevator pinged and the doors opened. The sound ricocheted inside her skull. Chastity let her step on first. "Stop being sarcastic. It doesn't suit you." Like the flip of a switch, Chastity smiled sweetly as she punched the buttons for the sixth and top floors. "So you finally got laid? Tell me all about it."

She smoothed the deep crease forming between her eyes. "Chastity, handling my professional business doesn't give you the right to delve into my personal business."

"You are my business." Chastity gave her another head to toe once-over. "From the looks of you, I'd say he had the whites of your eyeballs showing."

It was so close to the truth, Kamaria had to crack a small smile. "No comment."

"'No comment,' my ass. That smile you're trying to hide speaks volumes. What I want to know is why didn't you stick around for the breakfast round?"

She'd been asking herself the same thing ever since she snuck out of Jack's bed.

Because "the morning after" is always awkward.

Because I don't need to get in the habit of picking up strangers as a crutch for dealing with my problems.

Because it felt too right snuggled within his arms. No, she would not play Dr. Phil with Chastity this morning.

"Because he was too nice of a guy…"

"'Because he was too nice of a guy?' Do you hear yourself? Mari, you went through a lot and you've come so far. 'Too nice of a guy' is not a reason to push a man away. If anything, it's a reason to keep him close." Crap. Chastity was totally channeling Dr. Phil. Just because she sold self-help books, it didn't make her an expert on 'em.

"Yeah, well, you win some and you lose some, right? Maybe next time. For now, I'd like to be alone to get my mind right to finish this book." Chastity had meant well, telling her to find a guy and have a celebratory hookup. But with or without that advice, she'd been edgy, restless. Heading off one vice with another. She might talk a good game, but casual sex wasn't her thing.

Flashes of last night popped into her mind. Jack settling her on his couch so she could sleep off the tequila. Her pulling him down with her and straddling him. Her unfastening his pants and lowering her head…

"Jesus, I slept with the first guy who looked my way. I'm such a slut." The all too familiar twinge of guilt sank lower in her gut. "Celebrating with random sex? Chas, that was a stupid idea. I don't know why I listen to you."

"You listen because I'm always right. And kudos for trying to pin this on me, but you and I both know I'm not to blame. Mari, you *only* do what you want to do. Although I'll gladly take credit for this one."

"If sarcastic doesn't suit me, being smug is even less attractive on you."

"Puh-lease. You've been living like a monk for the last three years. You write about romance but you're scared to have any of your own. It isn't healthy. You achieved a major accomplishment yesterday and you let yourself have a little fun. You're a grown woman—there is no reason not to enjoy yourself as one. And you did it without having to gamble. That's a big step forward. I'm proud of you."

Kamaria rolled her eyes. Her agent had her best interests at heart. She knew that. And she couldn't blame her hottie hookup on anyone but herself. She'd wanted him. She'd pushed. He'd bit. Then nibbled. And sucked…

Any guilt she felt was totally worth the last few hours she'd spent with Jack.

The elevator stopped at Chastity's floor. "Get out of here. Before you bust out into song." She wouldn't put it past Chastity to start belting out "the hills are alive with the afterglow of orgasms…" Wait, she totally needed to use that line in a book.

Chastity stepped out of the elevator. "You're going to beat yourself up about this now, aren't you? Maybe I should come to the suite with you."

"No, I'm a big girl. I think I can manage a shower without running back downstairs for a hand of poker." Kamaria jammed the button to close the door a few times. With her other hand, she shoved the poker chip back into her pocket. She was a grown woman. Damn it. What did it take to be treated like one again?

"Call me if you need me—" The elevator doors shut in Chastity's face.

She pulled up the special calendar app on her phone. The tally count showed 1223 days. There had been times when she would drive as far as the halfway point between her home in Arizona and Las Vegas before she managed to talk herself into turning around. That's how strong the urge to gamble again had become. In the early days of her battle against compulsive gambling, she'd sold her car because fighting off the urge to drive the 250-mile distance had become too hard.

How was she going to fight it off when the casino was now one short elevator ride away?

Chapter Two

Jack Alderisi threw his phone onto the empty side of his bed. As if his day couldn't get any worse…

Ben had promised him he wouldn't be needed to work security at the Masquerade this weekend, but there was some damn romance novel convention at the hotel. Horny women were supposedly running amuck throughout the casino chasing half-naked men. Half-naked people wasn't really anything out of the ordinary for Sin City, but still…

Now, Ben was begging him to come in for a "special assignment." What kind of crap was that? Jack never should've answered the phone. He should've told the truth and said he'd had a very late night. Then he could've stayed in bed with the pretty, brown-eyed woman he had met—if only she hadn't snuck out while he was sleeping. He should be hauling her back to his bed instead of dragging himself into the cramped security office.

He was finally free of other people's responsibilities in his life. He could indulge his own desires for once. Right now, he desired tracking down his missing wild woman. She hadn't been wild in a swinging-from-the-ceiling kind of way, but he had found her bold, enjoy-the-moment-with-me-now approach insanely refreshing. He liked her combination of impulsive and sweet. She made him feel like it was okay to be impulsive. He needed more of that in his life. He had hoped to have more of that with her—for more than a few hours.

Jack pushed himself into a sitting position. The movement made him see stars. He added "hangover" to his list of reasons why his day was going to suck as he made his way toward the bathroom. He felt a smooth, cool piece of fabric under his foot. He knelt down to inspect the dainty garment. His mouth tugged into a smile. She'd forgotten what was left of her panties. Where he came from, when a woman left something behind, it meant she wasn't done with you yet. Jack entered the shower with a little more pep in his step. Maybe Fate was on his side for once.

An hour later, he was still pondering his missing bed partner as he walked toward the security office. He recalled her saying something about a book. What were the odds that she was attending the convention at this hotel? Would she reappear if he had her unique name paged over the convention floor intercom? His musings ended when he heard Ben's raised voice, "I'm sorry, ma'am. But it's not that simple."

Jack stopped in his tracks and began inching his way back out. But Ben's pleading eyes stopped him before he could get very far. Jack ran his fingers through his still damp hair.

"You're here. Great." Ben's desperate smile confirmed that Fate would definitely not be intervening where this "special assignment" was concerned. Ben never smiled. Jack really needed to stop being Mr. Always-Willing-To-Come-In-At-The-Last-Minute-Nice-Guy all the time.

"What do you mean it's not that simple?" The short, curvy woman seated before Ben jumped out of her chair and jammed her finger into Ben's chest. "There are hordes of fans—and I'm being modest here—who have saved up their hard-earned dollars and cents to come and stay in this hotel just to meet their favorite authors. Nobody here wants national, and possibly international, attention on how the new darling of bestselling romance fiction has a gambling problem. This plan is the only way!"

Ben backed away from the woman. "Ma'am, it's not our job to babysit gambling addicts. She needs a ticket on the next bus out of town, not a babysitter." Jack's mouth went slack-jawed. Ben locked eyes with him. "Help me out here, man."

The curvy woman whipped around. A wicked smile curved her lips as she took in the sight of Jack. He didn't like where this was going. If he ever did find his missing mystery woman again, he was tying her to the bed. "*You* are perfect. You look exactly like the cover model on her book. Are *you* free?"

"Am I free to do what?" Jack folded his arms across his chest. Whatever Ben had been planning with this woman, it couldn't be good.

"You'd be my personal lifesaver." The woman pointed a manicured fingernail at Jack. "I need you attached to my client's side from now until she checks out on Sunday. Make sure she shows up where she's supposed to be during the convention…" The woman cut a side-eye in Ben's direction. "And keep her out of the casino."

"No." Jack watched as both sets of eyes rounded in alarm.

"B-but…" the woman sputtered.

Jack shot Ben an angry look. True, Ben had once saved Jack's life back when they were in the Marines. A favor he could never fully repay. But, Ben knew better than to drag him into some shit like this. "Honestly, what Ben told you is right. She has no business being in this city, much less this hotel."

"I agree with you. I tried to tell her to wait for another convention in another city. But she's determined to prove to herself that she's kicked the habit." The woman's eyes darted to the security monitors. Jack watched as her mouth flattened into a firm line. All the fire that had been in her eyes immediately fizzled out. "Dammit, she's already on table four."

Jack's head followed the woman's pointed finger toward the monitor. The picture wasn't clear but Jack knew one thing for sure. He recognized the slouching figure on the screen. Oh did he ever. His hand moved of its own accord into his suit jacket pocket, his fingers rubbing the scrap of satin.

It looked like he'd be playing bodyguard this weekend. Fate had played Her hand. Luckily, he would be guarding the one body he wanted under his charge.

"I'm out." The puffed-up rapper wannabe across from her threw down his cards, shaking his head. Kamaria's heartbeat thudded inside her rib cage. She bit her lip to stop the smile. The action was the lone visible crack she allowed in her poker face.

"And the lady wins another five thousand!" The breath she didn't know she was holding whooshed out of her mouth. She threw the garbage that had been her hand—a pair of twos, a five of clubs, a four of spades and a queen—atop the pile of cards so the dealer could shuffle for the next round. She pressed her palm into her knee. With the other hand, she reached into her pocket and stroked her lucky poker chip. Whew. She still had the ovaries to play with the big boys—and win.

Just one more win and then she could walk away. No, she *would* walk away. Really, that's why she'd sat at the table in the first place. To prove to herself, to Chastity and anyone else who doubted her self-control that she could start and stop. That she could control herself. Problem was, this was the biggest gamble she could ever take, and any good player always knew when to fold 'em and walk away while she was ahead. Yeah, and if she was smart, she wouldn't walk, she'd definitely *run*. The long-buried urge, the oh-so-tempting high of the game, clawed its way from deep within her. God, it was a rush. Being a winner was everything. One last hand and she was done.

A hand dropped on her shoulder, causing her to jump. The sudden movement yanked Kamaria back to the here and now. She saw the last 1223 days fade into nothing. Her hangover headache started pounding behind her eyes with a vengeance. What the hell was she doing?

Oh God, what had she *done*?

"Ma'am, I need you to come with me."

Shame kept her locked in place, eyes down, trembling hands locked between her knees. She stared at the backs of her fingers, fighting that itch to touch her chips, the cards, to rub the felt of the poker table. Dammit, this wasn't supposed to happen.

"Ma'am." The voice was softer now.

"I didn't do anything wrong." The words were meant to convince herself. There might be a pile of chips in front of her, but she felt like a loser. Again.

"No one said you did." The man's hand now found its way between her shoulder blades. The warmth of his hand flooded into her. His warmth felt safe. Just like the guy from last night. She shook him off again. The last thing she needed was to be thinking about Jack. Or how she should've stayed in his bed. If she hadn't run from him, she wouldn't be here now.

"My associate Ben will take care of your chips for you. He'll have your winnings and the paperwork ready for you by the time we're done talking."

His voice was too smooth. Too practiced. Too, too familiar. Kamaria didn't like that either. She didn't even want the money. No amount of winnings could compensate for what she'd just lost by sitting down at this table. And talk? What could he possibly want to discuss? "I've got nothing to say to you. I was just leaving anyway."

The pressure on her back returned, this time more insistent. "That's where you're wrong, *Kamaria*. I think you have plenty to say to me."

She could tell by his emphasis on her name that he was going to kick her out. She'd ruined her sobriety, and now she'd messed up the conference too! She felt tears rim her bottom lashes. She willed herself to keep her chin up as she stood. This was no way to start her week at the convention. She had managed to stay away for so long. She hadn't even been in town sixteen hours and had already crumbled in the face of weakness more than once. All the promises she made to Chastity—to herself—about being able to avoid the casino evaporated into nothing. She should have never come back here.

The rent-a-cop's hand had now moved from her back to her arm. His grip tightened slightly, pulling her to her feet. The motion made her drop her lucky chip. She began to kneel but he was quicker. He snatched up her chip before she could retrieve it.

"Hey, that's mine. That chip doesn't belong to the casino. It's special."

Her stomach fell to her knees the moment the security jerk stood up so she could finally get a good look at him. The big, big body. The impossibly wide chest. Those full lips. Kamaria groaned. "Oh no, not you."

"Not another word." By now, Jack's hand was on her arm. His grip tight.

"Hey!" She tried to jerk away from him again.

"In my office. Now." Jack all but yanked her to his side.

Ben gave Jack the side-eye as he finished scooping the rest of her chips from the table. "Hey man, you don't have to rough her up like that. That wasn't part of the plan."

Jack held up a finger as he started to walk away with the woman in tow. Worming their way through the crowded floor, the height difference between them was more apparent now than when they had been in bed. His six feet and five inches to her…maybe five foot two. How in the hell had they fit together so well? It was a miracle he hadn't crushed her.

"Look, had I known you worked here, I would've never…"

Jack stopped in front of the service door at the back of the casino. He stopped himself just short of shoving her against the wall. The one time he allowed himself an after-work drink… The one night he decided to cozy up to a stranger. To take the offer thrown at him. He never loosened up like that. It might be Vegas, but his days of partying hookups were long behind him. But there had been something about this woman. Her personality, her blunt attitude, the way she'd wax poetic about something and then curse like a sailor. She'd made him want to take a leap for once. Oh, they'd taken the leap, all right. Straight into the fire.

"You would've what?" he muttered. "Not had the best orgasm of your life? Save it, honey."

He tugged her through the open doorway. A few turns along the nondescript hallways and they were in the security office. Jack pointed at the beat-up office chair. "Sit."

He handed her the crumpled panties from his pocket. "I believe these belong to you."

She bit her lip as she took the garment from him. She

looked up at him with those eyes. Those big, rounded eyes that had sucker-punched him in the gut the night before. Despite this disastrous turn of events, Jack still wanted her. He shook it off. "I'm not falling for that puppy-dog-eyed shit again. Spill your story."

She opened her mouth to speak but Jack cut her off. "The real story. All of it." Did he have a right to interrogate her? To haul her fine ass through the casino like she was some common card-shark or hustler? Well, no. But if he had any hope of helping her, of dealing with the next couple of days, she'd have to give it to him straight. His old man had had a gambling problem, too. Pussy-footing around his problem hadn't helped him in the end.

"You owe me that much," he said. He searched her face for a sign that he had affected her as much as she affected him. Her blank expression hit him like a sledgehammer. *Damn.*

The woman finally plopped herself down on the chair. She fiddled with the strings on her hoodie for a moment, then sighed. "My name is Kamaria Wilson. I like to gamble."

Jack jammed his eyes shut. The hope he'd been holding in his lungs deflated. It really was going to be a long day. "Fine, you're a gambling addict."

"I didn't say I was an addict. I might play too much sometimes. I'm not so out of control that I'd mortgage the house. But I *do* admit that I have a problem knowing when to stop."

At least she recognized she had a problem. That was good, right? His old man had lived in constant denial, gambling away their home and any hopes of his kids going to college. The only reason Jack had started picking up shifts at the Masquerade was so he could pay for his little sister's college tuition.

Kamaria ran her fingers through her twisted hair. She looked so defeated, Jack almost wanted to wrap her in his arms again. Almost.

"I didn't want to go in there today," she whispered. "I hadn't played a hand in over three years. But I have to be at a convention here this weekend. So I found the one bar in this town that didn't have any gambling in it. And then my agent called and said I hit the New York Times bestseller list. I wanted to celebrate, but the only way I know how to party involves gambling. I felt like such a loser. And then you started talking to me and we had that connection. So I did that, that whole thing with you last night instead. What can I say? Between you being so friggin' hot and…nice, and my having to be here, you made me feel safe."

"I made you feel safe?" Jack repeated. "That's why you snuck out of my bed?"

He paced in front of her chair. What he wouldn't give to be back at that dingy bar away from all this casino shit. Yeah, he shouldn't have ever answered Ben's call this morning. His home renovation business was taking off. His sister was graduating from college in a few weeks. He didn't need the extra money from this gig anymore. But if he hadn't answered, he wouldn't have found her again.

If only he hadn't been so out of his mind over this woman. The sex had been phenomenal. And he had held her close afterward, her head tucked on his chest as she snuggled so tight it was as if she couldn't get close enough. Sure, their connection had been unconventional and unexpected, but he'd closed his eyes and breathed in the scent of her thinking when they woke up, maybe, just maybe, they could see where things might go. That weak-ass thought flew right out the window when the woman literally flew out of his bed.

"I'm not responsible for you sitting down at that poker table, Kamaria." No, if she'd stayed where she belonged—in bed with him—she wouldn't have fallen off the wagon, and he wouldn't be playing savior for another addict. "I'd only approached you to make sure you were okay. You were the one hitting on me with the nightcap offer."

"You're gorgeous. A nice guy who knows how to use his tongue. What woman wouldn't get weak?" Her mouth curved into a shy smile. "Don't let the tongue part go to your head. Either one of them."

Too late. Jack smiled anyway. Dammit, the last thing he wanted her to know was that she amused him. Maybe even embarrassed him a little. Not that he would tell her that. But he never could hide his emotions. Everyone said his face was like an open book.

"If you had such a great time, why did you leave?"

Her expression blanched from toasty bronze to chalky brown. She gulped. Now she was the one who looked embarrassed.

"Because I don't know how to do 'the morning after,'" she whispered.

Jack chuckled to himself even though he knew that wasn't the entire truth. That spark, whatever it was between them, she had felt it, too. And now they had the rest of the weekend to see if that spark could be fanned into a flame. Her eyes narrowed as he coughed back the rest of his laughter. She looked so cute, like an angry Cabbage Patch doll.

"Stop laughing at me."

Crap. Pissing her off was the last thing he wanted. "I'm not laughing at you. I'm laughing because I don't know how to do 'the morning after' thing either."

Ben and the agent lady walked in at that very moment. Of course they did. Sonofabitch. As soon as Ben laid eyes on Kamaria in the chair, his expression transformed from his normal easygoing manner to hardened, badass cop mode. Jack watched as Ben let the door handle slide from his fingers, causing the door to slam shut. Kamaria damn near bolted out of her chair. "I'm sure Mr. Alderisi has been very accommodating in my absence…"

"Ben, wait," Jack started, but Ben held up a hand, not even sparing him a glance. Ben lived to play the bad cop role. What's worse, the agent had come up with this bullshit plan to frighten her and threaten her out of gambling.

"Well, playtime is over," Ben continued.

Ben swept in and spun Kamaria's chair so she was forced to look at him. Ben had done this routine dozens of times, the silent staring, admit-what-you-did-you-scumbag routine. Only this wasn't some common thief, or some asshat picking wallets while tourists were too entranced by all the shiny lights. This was an innocent woman—well, the things she'd done with her tongue last night hadn't been exactly innocent—but Kamaria wasn't a suspect here.

They might not be much more than strangers that had burned a couple of hours between the sheets, but knowing her story, he wasn't about to see her bullied for something she so obviously regretted. "Knock it off, Ben. It's not that serious…"

As far as Jack knew, treating her like a criminal wasn't part of the plan. Pulling her off the casino floor—that seemed to shake her up enough already. But now that they were in private, he was not cool with where this whole fake interrogation was heading.

But as it turned out, Kamaria didn't need his help. From the pile of chips he'd seen when he collected her at the table, he'd surmised she was good at cards. From her unflinching stare-down with Ben—no small feat, hardened felons withered under his stare—he realized she had the poker face to earn those winning hands. Damn, if it wasn't impressive. For once, someone was putting Ben's arrogant little ass in its place, and Jack was loving every minute of it.

And then, she released a gut-bucket chortle right into Ben's smug face. "Are you for real?" she asked. "Is this some good cop, bad cop foolishness you saw on some horrible incarnation of CSI?" Kamaria flicked her head to glance at her agent. "Who is this guy?"

Jack finally spoke up. "This guy is the head of security."

For the first time, a flicker of fear flashed across her face. From what he had seen so far, Kamaria had a shell so thick that only a hatchet could splinter it. She had no idea that a backdoor scheme had already been worked out for her benefit.

"Chastity, don't let them kick me out." A big fat tear slid down her cheek. Oh no, she was crying. Jack hated when a woman cried. He never had any idea what to do. Kamaria sniffed while shamelessly wiping away the tear. "I wasn't cheating. I wouldn't cheat. The only reason I'm here is for this conference. Tell them, Chastity."

Jack handed her a tissue. That was the not asshole-y thing to do, right?

"I'll find a way to stay out of the casino," Kamaria said. "I promise. Please don't ban me."

Jack gave her an awkward pat on the back. This ruse had gone far enough. "No one is kicking you out of anywhere. We've already decided that I will be your escort for the rest of your stay."

Her big, beautiful eyes lost some of their sparkle. "A babysitter, Chastity? I told you I wanted to handle this on my own."

"And I told you I would always have your back. I admire that you've come this far on your own. But, face it, hon, this time, you need help." The energy in the room shifted.

He hated watching her shoulders slump like a foundation about to crumble. There was a determination in her that his old man never had. He wanted to shore it up with his own hands if that's what it took to get her through this weekend.

The agent lady cleared her throat. "Gentlemen, I need a

moment alone with my client."

Ben waited until both he and Jack exited the office and the door had closed behind them. "I thought you were against this idea."

"I changed my mind when you started acting like an asshole." Jack hardened his features to let Ben know he didn't want to discuss it further. His buddy no longer had any say in Operation Save Kamaria. Ben got the hint.

"You playing babysitter is the perfect solution." Ben slapped him on the back. Ben's condescending tone made him bristle. "I'll double your normal rate for the trouble."

"No." Jack shook his head. It didn't feel right taking money to be by her side day and night. Not for what he had in mind. "This one's on me."

Ben's eyes widened. "I've never known you to pass up a dime. I guess your construction business really is back in the black."

"Yes, my business is back on track. Which you already knew because I told you *yesterday* not to call me for any more shifts. But that's not it."

"Oh, I get it. You like her." Ben nodded toward the door and licked his lips. "Yeah, that one has some fire. Her agent does too."

He squeezed his hand into a fist. *He saved your life. He saved your life.* He uncurled his hand. Still, he didn't like where Ben was taking this conversation. "She and I have unfinished business. Leave it at that."

Ben stepped back and held up his palms in defense. "Whatever, dude. I'm just happy you're willing to help me out. Besides, it's only three days. She's a little ol' thing. How much trouble could she be?"

Jack's mouth fell into a tight line. Unfortunately, he already knew just how much trouble Miss Kamaria Wilson was going to be.

" Jack is him?" Chastity gestured toward the door. "As in last night *him*?"

Jack. The name suited him. Strong. To the point. No fluff. And it sounded totally sexy when she'd screamed it while she came.

The office door opened before Kamaria could get out another word. Her eyes connected with Jack's. His eyes were on her as intently as they had been last night. Their one encounter clearly had not been enough for him either. She looked at the floor. This man was trouble for all the right reasons. "Follow me, ladies."

She felt safe again. She would gladly follow him anywhere. Preferably back to his bed. That was the problem. Shouldn't she be mad at him for appointing himself her savior without consulting her first? The last thing she needed, on top of everything else, was some self-appointed, alpha-male knight-in-shining-armor. "Actually…"

Chastity pulled her through the doorway. "Mari, don't say another word. You're over-thinking things again. Look at him. My gut says this guy is your real life hero."

In that moment, she was glad Chastity had badgered her into becoming her agent.

She watched him scratch the back of his head as he walked. The movement emphasized how snug of a fit he had inside his suit jacket. Dear Lord, the man had a set of guns on him, and not the kind that shoot. Maybe going along with this cuckoo plan wouldn't be so bad…

But there was one problem. Chastity was liable to let anything fall out of her mouth. When it came to a good tidbit of gossip, she would never let it die.

Ever.

She grabbed Chastity's arm and started to rush past Jack

and Ben. "Let's just go," she mumbled.

She took a quick glance back in Jack's direction and her stomach flip-flopped. He mouthed the words "I got you." Damn. He *was* a decent guy. Another shoulda-woulda-coulda. She turned back toward Chastity who, from the rueful smile on her face, had observed the entire moment that had passed between them.

"No, I'll lead you out." Jack walked purposely ahead of them, brushing Kamaria in the process. "Navigating these hallways can be tricky."

Correction, a decent guy who was also a gentleman.

"My word, he has a nice ass." Chastity's filter had left the building. Great.

Jack almost stumbled as he turned around. He gave them both a funny look before his long legs carried him ahead of them.

She groaned. "I don't know why I bother telling you anything. The word 'discreet' doesn't exist in your vocabulary."

"What's the problem?" Chastity pried her fingers from her arm. "There's enough sexual tension simmering between you two to totally justify another roll in the sheets. Am I right?"

Like she would admit to fantasizing about re-enacting the closet scene from *Scandal* in that tiny security office? She watched his deliciously round, firm ass continue to stride ahead of them. How could she resist not one, but now two major temptations this weekend?

"Have you asked him for some more yet?" Chastity taunted.

She swore she saw the tips of Jack's ears perk at Chastity's declaration. "Can you be any louder?"

"Girlfriend, I didn't get you on the New York Times bestseller list by keeping quiet." Chastity's grin spelled trouble. "This might be the best thing for you."

Kamaria shook her head and slowed her steps. She tugged on her hoodie strings and studied the tile patterns on the floor. On one hand, she appreciated Chastity's distracting comments. And she knew her agent well enough to know that the loud, suggestive remarks were meant to lighten the mood, but, the truth was, she had failed herself. She was back at day one. No, more like hour one. There was no way to get back those prior 1223 days of sobriety. Tears stung her eyes. Why would a nice guy like Jack want anything to do with a loser like her?

In all honesty, he probably saw her as *worse* than a loser because she needed a 24/7 guard at her side to keep her out of the casino. How pathetic was that?

While her lapse proved she couldn't do this on her own, maybe the best thing was to ignore whatever she was starting to feel for Jack. If they wound up back in bed together, it needed to be strictly physical. No emotions allowed. Between the pull of the casino and her overdue book, she already had enough on her plate. No sense in setting herself up for even more failure.

"Lightning has struck twice, Mari." Chastity stopped just before following Jack back into the hotel lobby. "I've worked my magic. Now, it's time for you to work yours."

"She's all yours now."

Jack willed his face to be stone still. This agent lady was a piece of work.

"Is that clear?" she pressed. "I expect you to be on Kamaria night and day."

Maybe he could've overlooked the first innuendo, but there was no mistaking the sexual overtones of that last one. The woman even added one of those suggestive eyebrow wiggles. Jesus. He began praying to every known religious deity and all of his Nonna's Catholic saints for this woman to stop talking. He felt feverish he was blushing so badly.

"But from what I've seen so far," the agent went on, "my gut tells me you can handle her and that you're the right man for the job. My gut is never wrong." She leveled her gaze on him in a way that definitely let him know that no pun had been intended. This time. Kamaria, on the other hand, was busy studying the popcorn plastering on the ceiling. Her normally tan cheeks had a faint pink flush to them. Maybe what she really needed was to be saved from her agent.

"Mr. Alderisi will escort you back to your room, Ms. Wilson," Ben said. "This will be the last time you are permitted on the casino floor. Understand?" That had been the sassy agent's decree. So at least on some level, it seemed she was honestly interested in helping Kamaria. Ben was still running with the scheme. Did the hotel give two shits about a gambling addict—uh, no. The billion-dollar empire was dependent on people like Kamaria. Jack held the door open for the ladies, allowing them to file into the main lobby.

"You know you're an asshole, right?" Jack flicked his wrist so the door would slam shut behind him.

But Ben managed to slip his foot in the door before it shut. "You're not fooling anybody, Poker Face. You like her." Then, the bastard had the nerve to laugh. "And she likes you."

Jack cursed under his breath and hurried to catch up to the women.

Unfortunately, that got him within earshot in time to hear the crazy lady ask Kamaria, "How soon do you think it'll be before you're in bed with him again? I'd give anything to have someone that gorgeous fall in my lap. And now, you're lucky enough to have his face in your lap twice."

"Chastity, I need you to grasp the concept of volume control." The faint pink tinge on Kamaria's cheeks darkened.

She was embarrassed, huh? Good. Now they were even.

"What are you talking about? I'm not being loud." Chastity's voice bounced off the walls of the lobby, turning heads.

"You're loud and your comments are lewd." She lowered her voice and he lengthened his stride to hear Kamaria whisper, "As for being with Jack again. That is none of your business." He caught that ever so subtle hitch in her voice. She was totally lying. Maybe there was a chance for them after all.

If he were a gambling man, now would be a good time to up the ante. The odds favored another pair of torn panties by nightfall.

Chapter Three

Chastity accompanied them into the elevator as far up as the sixth floor. Kamaria shoved the paperwork for her winnings into Chastity's hands. She'd handed over several thousand dollars. She should've been proud of her winnings, but she didn't want any access to that money. She didn't want to even look at it.

"I'll take care of this for you, my dear. Now, you kiddies enjoy yourselves. Tah tah!" Her fingers fluttered behind her as she exited the car.

"Jeez, how much did you tell that woman?" Jack mashed the button again for the tenth floor.

"Tell her about what?"

"About last night. Us."

"Oh yeah, that. Not much."

"'Oh yeah, that'? Seriously?" Out of the corner of her eye, Kamaria watched his jaw tighten. His deliciously broad shoulders got even broader. Then he leaned down and brushed her locks to the side. His lips mere inches from her neck. His breath tickled *that spot* on her skin, making her throb in all the right places. Was elevator sex legal in Nevada? "I distinctly remember you mumbling something about 'best orgasm ever.'" He breathed the words against her neck. She closed her eyes. *Do not shiver. Do not shiver.*

She turned her head. Now their lips were almost touching. "And wiping a tear from your eye," he continued. He swiped away an imaginary tear and then smirked.

God, he was entirely too gorgeous when he smirked like that. His dimples cut into his cheeks like deep lickable crevices. He was total hero material. Maybe she could convince him to pose for her next book cover. All big and bold and chivalrous. Everything she wanted her own fantasy man to be.

No, she had to resist his spell. For heaven's sake, she wrote romantic fiction, she wasn't supposed to be living it. She crossed her arms. "I had something in my eye."

"In addition to that best orgasm ever, I helped you out in a tough situation downstairs. You could start with 'thank you.' Or, how about, 'I'm sorry for banging your brains out and then leaving'? Had I known you had any kind of gambling problem, I would have never..." He paused and gently brushed her arm. She stiffened. Just as she suspected. A guy like him would never want to get mixed up with someone as messed up as her.

"...I would have never let you out of my arms. I woke up wanting to cook you breakfast. Make you scream my name. Again."

Her breath hitched. Why couldn't she come up with dialogue like that? This man wasn't just nice. He was perfect.

"So what do you say to a do-over, Kamaria?"

She shoved her hands into the pockets of her hoodie, determined to ignore his all too tempting offer. She liked the way he said her name. Said it correctly, too. She tried to force back a smile. He was making it harder and harder for her to think of him as just a fling. "Call me Mari. Everyone says it's easier."

Jack shrugged and moved his hand to the wall beside her head. "If I liked easy, I wouldn't be here. I prefer Kamaria. It feels better on my tongue." He licked his lips.

She shivered.

Dammit. She liked him even more. She had to figure out how to keep her feelings at bay around him.

The elevator pinged and the doors opened. Kamaria slipped through them as she marched toward her suite. Jack's long strides caught up to her in a few steps. "Wait, that came out wrong. I wasn't trying to get fresh with you. I really like the sound of your full name."

He didn't want to butcher her name? She could have swooned. "I…I know. Thanks."

She turned before he could see how his consideration affected her. She fumbled for the keycard in her back pocket. *This guy has to have some kind of flaw.*

Kamaria finally pulled out the keycard. "Back to your original question. The answer is not much."

"Not much what?"

"Chastity, my agent." She gestured back toward the elevator bay. "What I told her about us. I told her the gist of our night together when I got back to the hotel. And then when you found me in the casino, well, I had to tell her you couldn't escort me because you were *the guy.* All the other stuff was her taking that basic information and running with it. I swear that woman has a more vivid imagination than I do. You would think she was the creative one in our working relationship."

Jack caged her in with his arms against the door. "So you told her you like the way my ass looks?"

"No. She decided *she* likes the way your ass looks." *I, on the other hand, like the way you work it.* She wasn't going to tell him that, though. That would encourage him. She didn't need any more temptation. "Can I unlock the door to my suite now?"

"Of course." He stepped to the side. "But I feel like there's still weird energy between us."

Finally, a way to force a wedge between his hotness and her feelings. "Downstairs. You jumped in and called the shots like I'm incapable of making a decision on my own."

Jack's face fell. "We were ganging up on you. I saw it was stressing you out. So I made a decision to get you out of there."

"Thank you." Kamaria looked at her feet. Now she felt like an ungrateful bitch. See, she didn't deserve a guy like him. "Just consult me next time."

"Fair enough."

"Let's go in and get settled," Jack said. "I hope you have a decent-sized couch in there."

Jack wanted nothing more than to scoop her into his arms and hide her away from the world for the next few days. He looked around until he spotted the ceiling security camera that he knew was pointed right at them. He'd bet his next two bathroom upgrade jobs Ben was watching. Jack positioned himself so his body blocked Kamaria from the camera. He had a hard enough time keeping his wits about him where she was concerned. The last thing they needed was his old Marines buddy snatching a front row seat while they figured out this thing happening between them. But with this woman, maintaining control was already looking to be a lost cause.

Kamaria opened the door to reveal confirmation of Jack's biggest fear. Yes, she had a penthouse suite. But it was a junior suite. The smallest one on the floor. Which meant she had one California king bed and a living room furnished with a loveseat. Shit.

He followed her into the suite and locked the door behind him, sealing them away from prying eyes.

She looked him up and down from head to toe. All six feet five inches of him. She stared at the loveseat and then back at the length of him again. He liked that she absently licked her bottom lip.

"Well," she said, "the logical solution is to have you sleep with me…"

Jack plopped himself down onto the corner of the bed. "I think it's a great idea."

"Very funny. That loveseat is obviously too small for you. But…"

"We both know I'm too much of a gentleman to make you sleep on it. Little ol' you does not need all of that big-ass bed to yourself. The only logical solution is to share."

"There is always the floor." Kamaria's eyes sparkled back at him. That's it. He was hooked.

Jack rose from the bed and approached her. Her eyes widened, letting him know she wasn't nearly as unaffected as she pretended to be. "I thought you weren't mad at me anymore."

"I'm not," she stammered before looking away. It was downright adorable.

"Then what's the problem with me sharing your bed?" He couldn't even explain why this woman had him so ensnared. This was Vegas. She was from out of town. A one-night fling was to be expected. He wanted to help her. Okay, fine. Helping people was in his nature. But that wasn't it. There was something about her that made him want to be impulsive. With her. And for more than one night.

If she seriously didn't want him, no way would he push. But there was no denying the sexual energy between them. This guessing shit wasn't for him. If nothing else, she owed him some explanation. "Kamaria, I don't want to play games."

"Neither do I. Last night was last night. Today, in a way, is like us meeting for the first time." She cocked her head and mumbled, "Damn, that was good. I need to write that line down."

"I'll remind you," he said, before she could flounce off in search of a pen and paper. "Today's a new day. Fair enough. But why do you keep trying to push me away?" He towered over her.

"Jeez, you're like the alpha archetype, all big and pushy, rushing in to save the heroine from her train wreck of a life."

"We're not in one of your books, Kamaria." He wouldn't mind being her hero, for as long as it lasted, but something in her tone made him think she didn't believe she was a heroine who was worth saving.

"I can tell you're a good man, Jack. Too good for the likes of me."

Yeah. He'd hit that nail on the head. He cupped the side of her face. "I can be even better if you'd let me. We're stuck with each other for the rest of the weekend. Why not enjoy it?"

"Because you're a keeper and I wasn't trying to keep you. That's why I left." She pulled his hand away from her face.

"Wait, I'm not following."

"I only wanted one night. No strings attached. You're a nice guy. I don't deserve a nice guy for any longer than that."

He hadn't necessarily been looking for forever. If the time span was the issue… "Well, now, I'm offering you a weekend."

"No. I'd only be using you for sex."

Had sweeter words ever been spoken? "Then use me. You have my permission."

"Don't you get it yet? I'm screwed up. This connection we have? There's no point in exploring it further when nothing can come of it. You live here. Your job is here. We both know me in Vegas is a bad combination. You shouldn't get involved with a woman like me. I can't even handle avoiding a casino without someone following me around. I'm a loser."

"No, you're not a loser." Jack followed her into the outer room of the suite and watched her pace for a moment before taking a seat on the loveseat. He felt ridiculous sitting on the small sofa. Sleeping on it was definitely not an option. "I think you're brave."

She sighed. "Look, the last thing I want is for either one of us to get hurt when I leave on Sunday…"

If she thought she might get hurt then that meant she must care. Okay. He could work with that. He wouldn't push, but he'd be damned if he'd let an opportunity like this pass them by. They'd hit the jackpot with their random meeting last night and the explosive sex that'd followed. And he'd had his fair share of women. Enough to know that chemistry like theirs wasn't such a common thing. Then, getting called into work and assigned this babysitting gig? Yeah, that was another winning hand dealt to him. She might be willing to throw in the cards—and man, he *really* needed to stop with the Vegas metaphors—but he wasn't ready to quit just yet.

"Then you lay out the rules. I'll follow them." She said earlier she wanted to figure it out on her own. Fine, he'd just put that ball back in her court. "If by Sunday it looks like we could be something more, *I'll* deal with those roadblocks."

Her jaw dropped. Some of the tension seemed to leave her body. "I think I need a nap."

"Good idea. In the meantime, I'll ring housekeeping to bring up some extra pillows and blankets. I'll sleep on the floor. For now."

"Thanks." She pushed the sliding door to the bedroom shut.

Through the frosted glass door pane, he could see her peel her hoodie over her head. The curve of her ass and breasts silhouetted like a goddamn pinup when she turned sideways to slip out of her clothes.

A whole weekend without being able to touch this walking fantasy again? Shiiiit. He pulled the radio from his belt and pinged Ben's frequency.

"Ben, get me some pillows and blankets up here. And that picture of me with my Nonna on my desk. ASAP…"

Chapter Four

Jack could feel the tension in Kamaria build the closer the elevator car descended toward the bottom floor. He tried to pinpoint a particular trait about her that had drawn him in so quickly. It was that little glimpse of vulnerability, he decided. If not for the exact timing of meeting her in that bar, when her walls had crashed down or catching her at her lowest when she realized the damage she'd done by playing cards, he doubted he—or anybody else—would've seen that sensitive side. That softness she kept so hidden… It made him want to sweep her up and hold her close.

He wasn't buying her reasons for why they couldn't explore this thing between them. Gambling issue aside, he didn't buy her whole, "I'm not good enough" spiel. When he came back stateside after his second deployment, he'd been haunted by thoughts like that. It'd taken him some time to work through his baggage. To feel normal again.

His breakthrough had come when he moved out here to Vegas. Away from his Mama and Nonna smothering him, trying to fix his demons for him. Just like they had tried to do for his father, and failed.

Shit. That's exactly what he'd been doing to her.

Kamaria would never make peace with her demons, whatever they were, if he didn't back off. He could see that, unlike his old man, she wanted to face her issues with gambling head on, to move forward. But if he backed off, would he lose a chance at something more?

The more Kamaria fidgeted with nervous energy, the more Jack thought about stopping the elevator and pressing the button that would take them back to their own little heaven on high. He could back off later. This situation was exhausting for her, and he wanted to shake her agent for putting her in Vegas in the first place. Kamaria, being Kamaria, insisted on sticking it out and being here on her own. In his opinion, she didn't need to push him away. She needed his support.

"When we get out, stay to my right," Jack said. "My body will block you from seeing the casino entrance. Anytime you think you can't handle it, I can yank you outta there and back up to the suite." Dammit, he was doing it again. "That came out wrong…"

"I'm not some kind of poker crackhead." She had a determined look in her eye that he had to admire. "I've stayed away for over three years before this morning. Give me some credit. I don't even have access to any money to play with."

That left him stunned. He remembered from his dad's failed Gamblers Anonymous attempts that one way to help an addict was to have someone else handle all of their finances. She was trying so hard to stay on the straight and narrow. Whatever this was that he felt for her deepened with her admission. "Damn, I… Listen, I just want to make this easier for you. Help start you on day one of your next three years."

"I don't want to keep using you as a crutch. I've been doing too much of that already. I jumped into bed with you last night because you were a nice guy. You have manners.

You made me laugh. You made me forget…forget about…"

"I get it. Remember, I'm only trying to help."

"Thank you, but I'll never know if I can stand on my own two feet if you and Chastity keep 'saving me' before I have a chance to stumble. Yes, I fell off the wagon this morning. Now, let me figure out how to climb back on it."

Her words made his belly flutter with a serious case of like. He wasn't a fluffy romance kind of guy. What the hell was she doing to him?

The elevator stopped on the third floor and the doors opened. Two women got on, abruptly ending their exchange. The women were dressed in NASCAR-style racing jackets. The redhead looked him up and down and smiled. He discreetly stepped closer to the wall. The way she eyed him like a piece of meat made him uncomfortable. He looked to Kamaria for help. She was too busy smiling at the women to notice. The redhead elbowed her friend and loudly whispered, "Doesn't he look just like Antonio from the cover of *Race You for My Heart*?"

"Mary, don't be rude. He's probably one of the cover models."

"Well, don't he, honey?" The redhead was now looking at Kamaria. "Have you read *Race*…?" The woman gasped and clutched her chest, alarming everyone in the elevator. "Ohmigawd Susie. It's fucking Kamaria Wilson." The redhead started fanning herself.

Kamaria's face transformed into a bright smile and she held out her hand. "In the flesh."

"Wait, if you're Kamaria, then this really is the cover model from the book. OMFG, are you dating him? Don't shit me. Does this mean Antonio is real? That makes you Keisha. I knew it. That story was too real to be made up."

The friend pushed against Jack. He wasn't the claustrophobic type but, right now, he definitely couldn't breathe. "Did you two really do it on the beach in Monaco out in the open? Look at how gorgeous you are. Of course you did. How was it, honey? I've always fantasized about doing it on the beach. How do you keep the sand from getting in all your nooks and crannies?"

Thankfully, the elevator pinged its arrival on the lobby level. Kamaria grabbed his hand and yanked him off the elevator. But not before the frisky redhead pinched his ass. Kamaria pulled two cards out of her bag and handed them to the women. "Use the code on here to download advanced reader copies of my next book."

Both women squealed. "Can we get a picture with you and him?"

"Sure. C'mon, Jack."

The ladies flagged down a passerby to snap pictures with their smartphones. While they were hugged up, the redhead swiped a feel of his ass. Again. He grabbed Kamaria's hand and pulled her away. "Let's go."

Waving back at the women, Kamaria said, "Thanks, ladies. See you at the signing!"

Once they were out of sight of their elevator compadres, Jack grabbed Kamaria by the shoulders. "Excuse me, what was that back there? 'How do you keep the sand out of your ass while screwing on the beach?' Who asks a stranger that? Who is Antonio?"

"Antonio is the hero from my second book. He's an Italian race car driver. The story was set in Monaco. He and the heroine do it on the beach. That scene is a fan favorite." She looked particularly proud of that. "You do favor that cover model a little bit. Are you sure you've never modeled before?"

"No, never. I was in the Marines right out of high school and until right before I moved out here." Jack ran his hand down his face. "So you're telling me that all five thousand of these women will be harassing me all weekend because I look like the shirtless idiot on a book cover?"

"Yep, basically. Maybe not all five thousand of them. Not everyone here has seen the book."

As they approached the ballroom, Jack's breath caught in his throat. Chastity was rolling out a ten foot banner of a book cover that had a smiling face somewhat similar to his own on it. "It looks like they'll all see it now. I definitely didn't sign up for this."

He ground his teeth together to keep him from saying something he knew he would regret. He looked back at the elevator bay. They could go back upstairs and order room service for the rest of the weekend.

"Jack, there's no turning back now. The signing starts in a few minutes. You see all these ladies running around here. They're not going to be too happy if the authors, who they were told were going to be here, are not in their spots when the doors open. And I bet those ladies from the elevator are running their mouths about how the real life Antonio is here with me. If you don't go in there with me, they might riot."

Jack backed off with a harsh laugh. "Those ladies pinched my ass."

"I don't blame 'em. It's a fine ass. You have to go in there with me now. It's not safe for you to walk the floor alone. You think getting your butt pinched was bad? They're liable to jump you if I'm not around to keep them at bay."

"That's ridiculous."

"You said you wanted more of me. Well, welcome to my crazy." Kamaria held out her hands. Forget her demons. He was beginning to think this was why she had tried to push him away.

"Besides, I need you here. You keep me calm. When you're around, I don't think about wanting to play cards." She lifted her head to look up at him through her lashes. "I don't feel weak."

Jack could tell that wasn't an easy confession for her to

make. She had him there. He thought of all the times his old man had gambled away everything without remorse. At least Kamaria was trying to do the right thing. If she somehow wound up back at the poker tables, he'd never forgive himself.

"Fine. But if my ass gets pinched one more time…"

Kamaria reached around and pinched his butt cheek. "You'll what, spank me when we get back to the room?"

Jack rubbed his behind. "No, worse."

"Maybe I should grab that ass again. When we're alone." Kamaria winked at him as she sat down at the table with her name on it.

"I hope that means you decided to share the bed." He put his hands on her shoulders, giving her a gentle squeeze. She was flirting with him again. That was a good sign. Maybe he wouldn't have to sleep on the floor after all. "How long will you be signing books?"

"Until the line is gone. If a reader scraped together money to have me sign their books, I'll be here to do it."

Jack shook his head. "I still don't get it. They're just books. Words on a page."

"Not to these women. Not to me." She nodded her head toward the crowd waiting at the door and then gestured toward the other authors who were getting themselves settled. "For some of them, books are their only escape from their hectic lives. My grandmother had me read romance novels from the library to her when we didn't have enough money to keep the TV on."

She stared off for a moment. "After she died, reading her favorite romance books kept me sane. Then I moved on to writing them to honor her memory. That kept me occupied as I worked through the disaster that gambling too much had turned my life into," she said quietly. He felt a wave of sadness pass through her. He rubbed her shoulders a few times. The tension in her muscles challenged even his work-strengthened hands.

"Hey, forget what I said back in the elevator. I can't imagine what all this is like for you. You came here to your own detriment just to meet your fans. That takes a lot of guts. I gotta respect that."

Kamaria leaned back into his palms. Her eyes fluttered shut like she was savoring the moment. She stayed that way for a few seconds and then leaned out of his reach. "I only have a few minutes left to set up my station. Thanks for trying to understand. It helps."

Kamaria went into her bag to pull out her special purple markers. She wanted to smack herself in the forehead. She could have totally jumped him right here on the hotel ballroom floor. That type of impulsiveness was what got her addicted to gambling in the first place. She took a very slow, very controlled inhale. *I can do this. This is all for my readers.*

Yes, she used her readers to justify the crazy decision to come back into town, but the reality was that she had to come back here for herself. She and Chastity had a major fallout before accepting the invitation to come here. But she needed to see if she could do it—stay in control in the midst of every temptation, in every direction. Her grandmother would be so proud. True, she'd failed within her first twenty-four hours back in town. But she'd managed to survive. She hadn't tried to go back to the poker tables after Jack had found her. He made damn sure of that.

She wasn't kidding when she told Jack that he kept her calm. As fine as he was, he provided the distraction she needed to keep her demons under control. The odd thing was it wasn't always lust that drove her desire to be around him. Just his presence, even if in the sitting area of her suite, made her feel alive again. Her confidence began to overshadow her stage fright. Her word count flowed easier. Her plot twists and ideas had been more abundant. And that was only from sharing a room with him for a couple of hours.

The doors opened and the readers poured into the ballroom. A long line formed quickly for her. More than a few readers had contacted her on social media to let her know they would be there. But she never expected this. Not everybody wanted an autograph or a picture. Some stood in line just to stay thank you or to shake her hand. As she predicted, more than a few people "recognized" Jack as the cover model on that book. The way some of those women looked at him—he might as well have been wearing a thong instead of a suit. That made her stomach tighten with jealousy. Well, until Jack began asking her about what else this Antonio did besides bone some chick on the beach.

A female gasp broke her musings. "Oh-oh-oh, it's Antonio. Kamaria, girl, how did you manage to get him here without letting anyone know?"

"Actually, he isn't the same guy…" she started.

An older woman with honey-blonde braids tapped Kamaria on the arm with her rolled up program. "I hope you have a plan for getting him out of here. Once the masses get a hold of him, it is going to be a straight up problem in here. We might need to call casino security in to save you, young man."

Up until the woman said this, Kamaria had managed to keep a relatively neutral expression on her face. But the "casino security" comment, in combination with her nerves, basically destroyed what was left of her composure. Kamaria clapped her hands to her mouth, but that did little to cover her peals of laughter. "Girl," she whispered through her hands. "He *is* casino security."

She could see Jack's body tense out of the corner of her eye. More and more people had crowded around her table. Maybe the honey-blonde braids woman was right.

She saw Jack tap his radio earpiece and mouth the words, "We have a situation." The room temperature continued to increase from the amassed body heat of several hundred conference attendees. As the buzz about Jack spread, the crowd swarmed like bees to get a glimpse of him, jamming forward in a way that pushed her table a couple of feet. She shoved her chair back to compensate, but with a wall not far behind her, in a few more seconds, they would be trapped.

Jack leaned down to her and whispered, "We need to get out of here. Now."

He reached for her arm to help her up, but she pulled away. "You go. There are still readers waiting for an autograph."

"You can sign their books later. Right now, I'm trying to save your life."

She saw some random hand pinch Jack's ass. He jumped. She was out of her seat a second later, jealousy making her ball her signing hand into a fist.

"That's like the twentieth time. My ass cheek is completely numb."

His comment defused some of her jealousy and had her fighting the urge to laugh, but a glance around her at the crowd pushing closer and more aggressively had her agreeing with Jack's earlier assessment. They did indeed have a "situation."

The tension in the room was palpable. But then again so was the excitement. It was hard to gauge which way the energy would flow. Was this just a bunch of women having a good time? Or was this the calm before the storm? Another surge of the crowd and the table bumped into her, pushing her closer to the wall.

Jack wasn't taking any chances. "Kamaria, we have to go. Now."

She handed the book she had just finished signing back to its owner with a shaky hand. The woman gave Jack a shy smile, then thrust the book in his direction. "Would you sign it too? I never thought I'd get to meet Antonio in the flesh. You're way more gorgeous in person."

That one gesture turned the tide of the crowd toward chaos. A number of women in the vicinity had lurked around the table, trying to engage him. Once the woman asked for Jack's autograph, the others took that as permission to flock toward him.

"Ooh, I want an autograph too."

"Take a picture with me."

"Do me like you did Keisha in the book!"

The women mobbed around Jack, reaching, pushing, and, unfortunately, grabbing. This was bad. Kamaria felt like the world was closing in tight around her. Her breath caught in her throat. She used her short height to her advantage by ducking and reaching into the crowd for Jack's arm. When she finally caught it, he clapped his other hand on top of hers. She flexed her fingers into a death grip around Jack's hand.

Jack pulled her forward, but fear locked her legs in place. So he swooped his arms under her knees and across her back instead.

She made the mistake of blinking and missed the whole fairytale moment. One second they were in the bright yellow ballroom. The next they were in the purple and green hallway. Her attention immediately went toward the direction of the casino entrance. She could see there were only a few people there. It looked like a safe space. *Her* safe space.

"What about the…?" She began to twist out of his arms.

He tightened his grip, holding her closer to him. "No, look at me. Only look at me. I have you."

Jack elbowed them through the stunned crowd, away from the chaos. Kamaria shivered. "Stay focused, baby. We'll be out of here in a sec."

Look at Jack. Only at Jack. If not for her damned weaknesses, there was nothing, no one else she would want within her sights. His jet black hair, not short but not too long either. The way his beard framed his mouth. Oh, those lips and the things they did to her. The nose that had been broken at some point.

The determined look in his eye made her feel the safest she had been since she had last been this close to him. Had last been engulfed by his arms with him looming over her, stroke for stroke. His intent stare made her feel like the only thing in his world. She tucked her head under his chin and closed her eyes. He cradled her closer to his body, like a running back with an oversize football. Everything about this moment felt incredibly right. She had been wrong about the casino. *He* was her safe space.

She might have to kidnap this guy on her way out of town.

The sounds of the slots and the rest of the casino faded away. The vice-like tension around her torso loosened. Her pulse felt less like an imminent heart attack. They were in the lobby now, but Kamaria could tell they had passed the elevators that would take them back up to her suite. She pulled her head out of the crook of Jack's chin and looked around. "Where are we going?"

"I'm getting you out of here." Jack pushed through a more visible service door that led them back into a hallway very similar to the one outside of the security office. "Those ladies were trolling the area by the elevators. There's no way I'm getting stuck in close quarters with them again. Especially when you need time and some space to get yourself together."

"Good luck with that. There aren't many places in this city where I'm not going to be around something that would tempt me." *Especially with you attached to my side.* It had taken her almost two hours of searching the internet to find that dive where she met Jack.

Jack pushed through one last door. "I know. That's why we're taking the service elevator."

Chapter Five

Jack kept her in his arms until they were at the door to her suite. She took her keycard out of her pocket with a shaky hand. Jack took it from her and swiped it in the lock. "We're safe now. What do you need me to do, Kamaria?"

She relished having a moment where someone else took charge. She may have argued otherwise when he first came upon her with security, but that had just been her pride talking. Jack had "rescued" her then and he was doing it again now.

"Tell me what you need, baby girl."

She slid down his body until she was standing on her feet. What did she need? She needed him. But no... "I, uh, just need a few moments to process what happened."

"I can do that." He held out his hand to her. "Come with me."

She took his hand without hesitation. Those three words together could mean so many things. They could mean something as simple as coming inside the room or allude to a promise of more to come. But from what she'd seen so far, Jack wasn't one to hide his emotions. So she knew she could literally take his invitation at face value. And, right now, his face told her he was simply being a gentleman.

She had no good reason to be nervous. He wasn't leading her to a seduction. He wasn't some random hot guy she picked up at a bar anymore. Her emotions weren't cloaked by the fog of alcohol. He was Jack. This man had her on the verge of breaking her most basic rule regarding men within the first twenty-four hours of knowing her: don't get caught up. But, more and more, she found herself wanting more from this man than just sex. She did not need any reason to linger in Vegas past Sunday, nor a reason tempting her to return. But…

She tightened her grip around Jack's hand like the emotional anchor it was. It wasn't the fact that he was assigned to be her babysitter that kept her out of the casino. It was *him*. His mere presence made her feel like she might be not only good enough, but strong enough to kick her gambling habit for good. He made her want to be a better person.

"Have a seat." He guided her toward the loveseat. After settling her on the couch, he stepped back, took off his suit jacket and laid it over the arm. "I'll be right back."

He went into the bathroom without another word.

She could hear Jack puttering around. She assumed he was throwing some water on his face to give himself a moment to compose himself. That mob downstairs had been intense. It wasn't like he had anticipated being stuck on a babysitting detail requiring mob control when he reported to work this morning.

Kamaria was grateful to have this moment of quiet. She leaned back and closed her eyes. And tried not to think about how this could be an everyday scene of domestic bliss for them one day. Conflict sold books, not depictions of the actual "happily ever after."

Her brief semi-solitude was broken by the sound of

running water. She flicked one eye open. He must be one of the uber neat freaks, she mused. The type to obsessively wash if he even broke out into a single bead of sweat. Kamaria sucked her teeth. Finally! Something to make Mr. Jack Alderisi a little less perfect.

The next thing she knew Jack was gently pulling on her hand. "Come on. I have a surprise for you."

"Does this surprise have anything to do with the water I heard running?"

"You'll find out soon enough." Jack's mouth quirked into a mysterious smile. A flash of them naked and intertwined in the shower overtook Kamaria's imagination. The side of her face pressed against the cool tile as Jack slid into her from behind. She stumbled over an imaginary pucker in the rug. Jack's other hand reached for her arm. "Are you all right?"

Kamaria pulled her face into a well-practiced mask. "I guess I'm still out of it. The last twenty-four hours have been a little crazy."

"Then I feel even better about surprising you with this." Jack led her into the bathroom. The calming scent of lavender filled her nose. Jack leaned over the bathtub and turned off the faucet. "Take off your clothes."

"Excuse me?"

Kamaria searched his face. His eyes held no glint of humor. "You. Naked. In the tub. Take a break."

She stepped past Jack and gripped her clothes close to her body. "Okay."

"I put the bath salts from your welcome basket in the water." A proud grin spread across his face.

"Thanks." Dammit, he was back to Mr. Perfect again. They stood there staring at each other awkwardly for a few seconds. "Did you want to join me, or…"

"No, this is your time. There's a towel on top of the sink for you. Is there anything else you need before I step out?" Her insides fluttered. Now he was Mr. *Too* Perfect. Jack grabbed the door handle and backed out of the room. "Enjoy."

"Damn." She let out the breath as she wriggled out of her denim jacket. She looked back at the door from which Jack had exited. "That man isn't just perfect. He's a keeper."

Exactly the kind of man who didn't deserve to get swept up in her drama-filled life.

She lifted her dress over her head and chucked it onto the floor. The rest of her garments quickly followed. She lowered herself into the tub. The water sloshed around as she settled herself. The temperature was perfect.

She soaked for about twenty minutes before she pulled out the stopper. She still wasn't ready for the world yet. Now was as good a time as any to wash her hair.

Kamaria pulled out the few hairpins securing her updo. She got out of the tub and swiped her toiletries from the sink. As she entered the separate shower stall, she didn't miss the fact that it was big enough for two.

She turned on the showerhead and backed her head into the spray. With shampoo pooled in her palms, she wound her fingers through her locks and scrubbed at her scalp. Her homemade peppermint oil shampoo tingled as it worked through to her roots. Twisting her hair back into decent shape would take forever. Normally, she would balk at the task. But, right now, taking time to take care of herself was just what she needed.

Kamaria leaned back and let the showerhead rinse the concoction from her hair. What was she going to do about Jack? The way he had swept her into his arms had her walls crumbling. She could tell he wanted her again just as badly as she wanted him. But he had kicked into protective mode rather than taking advantage. She had no defense for that.

Sneaking out of his apartment while he had been asleep was supposed to avoid this very situation. One night of amazing sex. No strings attached. Even if she'd never set eyes on Jack again, she'd been tied to him. The night they'd shared was something she'd forever cherish. Not that she wanted to admit that, even to herself.

Once her hair was clean, Kamaria squirted some of her favorite jasmine-scented body wash onto a loofah. She started lathering her inner thigh, but had to stop as memories of Jack washed over her.

Turning her life into one of her romance novel plots had never been the plan...

It was just her luck that the chapters she needed to finish this weekend were the steamy ones. Maybe she should just type up all the things that Jack had done to her last night. Then, she wouldn't be tempted to spread her legs for him a second time.

Maybe it was time for her to look into a Gamblers Anonymous meeting. She'd blown three years of sobriety within the first twenty-four hours back in town, and she had three more days to go. See? Drama. But who wanted to sit in a room with a bunch of addicts when sexy-assed Jack Alderisi could be naked and ready in her bed when she stepped out of the bathroom? More sex with him was all the therapy she needed.

She slid open the shower door. She wrapped one towel around her head, another around her body, and moaned as its soft fluffiness embraced her. This had to be Egyptian cotton with a thread count of a bazillion or something. Now that she had officially hit the New York Times bestseller list, maybe she would splurge for a couple of these towels once the royalties started rolling in. She would have to ask Chastity about ordering some for her. Until then, enjoying all of the luxuries within this suite might make the torture of being in Sin City a little more tolerable.

She dried off the rest of her body and left the towels

in a heap in the middle of the bathroom. She drew on the thick purple robe left for her by the convention planners. It impressed her that they had gone out of their way to find one in her favorite color. Their attention to detail touched her and left her with a twinge of guilt that she had left the book signing like she had. She would have to find a way to make it up to them, and to the readers who had still been waiting.

She reached for the door leading to the bedroom. "I have to do better," she resolved, staring at her reflection in the giant mirrors. "I need to stop leaning on Jack as a crutch and figure out how to deal with being in Vegas on my own."

She stopped short of entering the bedroom and closed the door again. She was so lost in her thoughts that she had forgotten to grab the hair lotion and oil she needed to re-twist her damp locks. The sash on her robe loosened and fell as she grabbed the bag that held her hair care products. Just at that moment the door leading to the suite's living room opened.

Confused, Kamaria looked up into Jack's shocked face. Her toiletry bag slipped out of her fingers, further widening the gap between the already gaping robe lapels. Jack's gaze immediately zeroed in on her nudity. His eyes momentarily shone with desire. Silently, she urged him to make a move. There was no way she would resist the hungry way he looked at her. But then, the corners of his eyes crinkled with regret.

"I heard the door shut. I thought you were in your room. My bad." Jack swallowed. She watched his Adam's apple bob up and down. But he didn't look away. "You look great when you're naked."

Her breath caught at Jack's last blurted out statement.

"I'm an asshole for saying that."

She shook her head. "No. But, you do have a great ass."

"Isn't that what Chastity said?" Jack threw up air quotes. Now that his suit jacket was off, she could see how his biceps bulged under his dress shirt. Her new resolve to not use Jack as a sexual crutch was crumbling. Oh, who was she kidding, it was totally crushed.

"I never said I disagreed with her assessment of your backside."

Jack smiled. "I like that you like my ass."

And Kamaria liked it when he smiled at her like that. It made her swoony. Now wasn't the time to develop a swoony habit. "Jack."

"What?"

"Get out."

"Why?"

"I'm naked."

"You're wearing a robe."

Kamaria pulled the open edges of the robe together. "A robe that was wide open."

"I wasn't complaining."

Her attempt to frown failed. She allowed herself to return his smile. Why must he be so irresistible? "I think it's time to lay down some rules."

They came to her instantly.

Jack crossed his arms across his chest and leaned on the doorframe. "Lay it on me."

"One, we're together for the weekend only. When I check out, that's it." *Know when to hold 'em…*

"Fair enough." That surprised her. She had hoped he would object.

"Two, sex only. If either one of us starts catching feelings, it's over." *Know when to fold 'em…*

She prayed her face didn't betray her.

His frown said everything. He didn't like that caveat. "Is that all?"

Three, stop being such an amazing guy.

"Yes." *Know when to walk away…* She lifted her chin. "Do you agree to these terms?"

"Not really. But I'd like to add one more condition."

Wait, what? She felt more vulnerable than when her robe was wide open.

"A wild card, if you will. I'll play your game for now. But, when you finally admit that you like me, you know, *like that*, I get two more days. Outside of Vegas. Location, my choice."

"I don't like you *like that*, Jack."

"That's what you say now. I don't think either one of us believes it though."

Know when to run...

Shit. He'd just called her bluff. "Maybe this was a bad idea. We should stick with the original plan. You sleep on the floor and..."

"Push me away all you want. I'm not going anywhere."

He started to back out of the bathroom. His line of vision shifted from her body to her eyes. "Next time, make sure this door is locked if you don't want me to come in."

Kamaria took a deep breath. Her resolve to not be tempted by this man was completely gone now. She crossed her arms just beneath her breasts, propping them up. "What makes you think I didn't want you? To come in, that is."

"From what I know of you so far, you're a no bullshit woman. If you want something, you say it." He shortened the distance between them in a few steps. "Do you want me, Kamaria?" Jack grabbed her wrist. His fingers began stroking the sensitive flesh just beneath the padding of her thumb. He closed his eyes. "Should I assume that silence implies agreement?"

For a woman who made her living with words, she was shocked to find herself rendered speechless.

When she didn't reply, he said, "Do you really want this to end before it's begun?"

"No, I—"

His mouth swooped down to claim hers. His tongue

invaded her mouth and she quickly forgot her smart-ass retort as his hands flicked the terrycloth away, then encircled her waist. He yanked her hips flush against his thigh, then walked her back against the steam-slicked tile wall. Sweat beaded on her brow. He had the unobstructed access to go further, but held back. He was waiting for *her*. She lifted her hands from his shoulders, her fingers frozen with indecision. She *should* swat his hands away. But she *wanted*... So much for her plan of a cool and collected approach.

Her fingertips stroked the neatly trimmed whiskers of his beard. Oh, that beard. She shuddered as she remembered the scruffy feel of those whiskers against her sensitive inner thighs as he had nuzzled her intimately.

She *had* to be stronger than this...

With a sigh, she reached back and moved his hand lower. She could figure out how to be strong later. He groaned against her mouth, kissing her deeper. Yes. *Yes*. God, he took her to that mindless place. His hands streaked along her skin, massaging, exciting, enticing.

His lips were soft but persistent, his tongue doing things in her mouth that made her body hungry for so much more. Then his hands came up and framed her cheeks. His hands were large enough to cup her entire face. He kissed her tenderly, gently, with so much affection it made entirely different emotions boil up from deep within.

In the end, he backed away. He stepped back and let out a deep breath. "Get dressed, Kamaria."

"Excuse me?"

"I'm competitive by nature. You don't get to win that easily."

"But..."

"You have no problem putting everything on the line for some cards." Her robe had fallen open again. Jack pulled the two lapels together. "Why won't you take that same risk with me?"

"Careful, Jack, this is supposed to be sex only. Why not take advantage of the situation? Most men would."

One side of his handsome mouth curved upward. "Now we both know I'm not like most men."

"We agreed no emotions involved."

"Ah, yes, your rules. For a game neither of us truly intended to play." He knelt down, deftly retrieved her pouch of hair products and handed it up to her. "Just let me know when you're finished in here."

The door slammed shut behind him. Kamaria's knees gave out, causing her to slide down the wall until she sat on the cool tile floor. Her hands trembled, not from cold, but from fear. He was beginning to nudge his way into her heart. She needed to get a grip. If she couldn't stop herself from falling for Jack, would she ever be in control of anything again? *Focus on the little things. The things you can control.*

With more focus than was probably necessary, she took another breath. She needed to call Chastity and let her know that this crazy plan wasn't going to work. But first, Kamaria had to re-twist her hair. Something simple. A task within her control.

She made a big noisy show of opening the door to the bedroom and letting it slam shut. "It's all yours," she called out. Jack's lack of a response made her unintended innuendo hang that much louder in the silence. He was right, as badly as she was tempted to gamble again, that was the lesser of temptations. And if he nudged again, she really would be all his.

Chapter Six

It's all yours...

Jack shook his head. She was playing with him again. And damned if he didn't like it. He picked up his overnight bag. If she was still in the bathroom this time, all bets were off. It was already taking the patience of Job for him to maintain any semblance of control around her.

He pushed the bathroom door open. The room was empty. Thank goodness. He needed time alone to get his mind right.

The moment he closed the door behind him, the solitude he had hoped to have was gone. Her scent still hung heavy in the air. It was a combination of a sweet, flowery smell and peppermint. It invaded his nostrils. Caressed his senses. His entire body reacted to the assault. His hand slid from his belly down to beneath his waistband. He started to stroke himself but stopped. No. What was he doing? He was a grown ass man.

Damn. Never before had any woman so completely invaded his life. Or so quickly.

He made quick work of stripping and jumping into the

shower. A decidedly lukewarm shower. He put his forehead against the cool tiles. But his raging hard-on wouldn't die. He ran through the most non-sexual mental images he could think of. The check he wrote for his baby sister's last college tuition bill. His mama nagging him about the tuition bill even though he already paid it. His Nonna's nasty afterschool sandwiches.

Remembering those sandwiches did the trick. He felt himself begin to soften. He grabbed the closest washcloth and mopped his face. Bad move. Kamaria's scent assaulted him all over again. She'd washed herself with this soft cloth. His imagination flooded with images of all the places that washcloth had been. Twisted between her fingers. Spreading suds up the valley of her thighs. Around her belly. Circling her breasts. Everywhere his hands could have been just moments ago. Jack groaned. He was hard all over again.

He was in no mood to fight it any further. With a soap-slicked hand, he fisted himself. He grunted with every pull. When he came, he bit his forearm to muffle his moan. God, he hoped she couldn't hear him through the wall.

Three hours later, Kamaria lay in bed wide awake. Each soap-slicked slapping sound Jack had made during his shower replayed in her mind. The telltale moan that had accompanied his release. Her hand had been jammed against her core ever since. It should have been her hands pleasuring him. Her mouth receiving his release. No-strings-attached sex for the rest of the week shouldn't have been this complicated. Why was he being so stubborn?

On the other side of the French doors, she could hear Jack trying to get comfortable on the loveseat. The fact that a man his size would entertain the thought of sleeping on that thing was ridiculous. However, he had tried the floor first, but that wound up aggravating an old back injury. Now, his flopping around was keeping her awake. Each toss and each turn made her ultra-aware of his nearness. Each frustrated sigh reminded her of how he growled when he kissed her. And of how much she wanted him to kiss her again. Her mind went back to those damn rules. Liking his kisses was not the same as liking him, as he said, *like that.*

She had no problem using him again for sex. He'd already given her the green light for that. But that kiss... It had changed everything. Clearly, both of their emotions had ignited it. He knew that her emotions were already on the table. That's why Jack had issued her that challenge: admit she liked him and he gets two more days with her. No, sir. Why would he even say that to her? Come Sunday, she was outta there. That was a challenge she would not let him win.

But now, her need for competition had been stoked. She needed to play in some shape or form. If Jack wasn't game, then she should just go back to the casino.

No. She flopped onto her stomach and cradled a pillow between her arms. She kicked her feet against the mattress. She tossed herself onto her back and then she drummed her fingers against her chest. The tightness from earlier began to return. The bed was too big, too empty. Taking the California-king suite had been Chastity's idea, not hers. Chastity was used to this luxurious shit. Whereas she had spent the last three years learning again how to live without it.

The urge had never been so strong to play a hand. Just one hand. She thought about the fifty dollar bill she hid in her wallet for "emergencies." Didn't everything about her situation scream "EMERGENCY"? That bill surely was enough to be dealt into a decent round. Just once. This morning, she'd been able to get up. In fact, she'd been about to leave the table before Mr. Perfect swept in. Stopping hadn't been a problem then. It wouldn't be a problem now. As long as she didn't get caught.

She was back on day one anyway. She had nothing to lose.

Jack's breathing had become more even, more relaxed in the last few minutes. Kamaria sat up. She should go now while Jack slept. He wouldn't even notice...

What happens in the dark always comes to light. Her grandmother's words rang clear in her mind. She felt a guilty lump form in the pit of her stomach. Jack would never look at her the same if he caught her back in the casino. The way he'd looked at her when he told her she was brave, that made her feel like she could fly. Did he really want to fly with her?

That's it. She didn't want to think anymore. She wanted her mind to clear, to be on auto-pilot. Gambling did that for her. One last hand would quiet her mind. Get her into the zone. She could prove to herself once and for all that she could start *and* stop playing on her own. She swung her legs from under the covers and onto the floor. She began creeping through the dark, only to wind up fumbling and making more noise than necessary.

"What are you doing?" She froze. Jack's voice made her heart leap into her throat.

"Nothing," she croaked. Dammit. Could she sound any guiltier?

She heard him flail either his arms or legs from under the covers. A muffled thud. There was another thud followed by a curse. It sounded like it had been one of his limbs connecting with the coffee table. Finally, Jack flicked on the light in the living room.

She jumped back onto the bed. He yanked open the door to the bedroom. She was too slow in throwing the comforter over her body. There was no way Jack hadn't seen her jean-clad leg and sneaker-covered foot.

Jack, in all his rippled, shirtless, and red-boxer-brief-clad glory, stood over her with one eyebrow raised. "Going somewhere?"

The guilty lump in her stomach lurched. The weight of his judgment made her lungs constrict. She gulped. "Well, if you were in bed with me instead of trying to sleep on that ridiculous loveseat, I would be too distracted to go anywhere…"

Jack held up a hand, cutting her off. "Nice try. Face it, you've been a bad girl. Time to face the consequences."

Wait, did he just go alpha on her? Kamaria closed her eyes and counted to three before opening them again. Nope, her girl parts were still pulsing with desire. And really, wasn't this what she'd wanted from the start? For him to take charge. To make the decision for her so she didn't have to think or face the emotions she wasn't ready to feel…

"The only reason you would try to leave is so you can go downstairs and gamble. Well, that ain't gonna happen, sister. Not on my watch."

Jack turned his back to her. He went back toward his makeshift bed and started digging through his overnight bag. This gave her an unhindered view of his very perfect ass. Two round globes encased in his underwear that made her palms itch to grab him. *He's not a globe, Kamaria. He's a man. A man with feelings…*

"I'm guessing you have an itch that needs some serious scratching…"

He turned around. She felt her eyes widen. *He's a man with an incredible hard-on. For you.*

Jack dangled a pair of handcuffs from his fingers. She scrambled back against the headboard. "Jack, don't you think that's a bit drastic? Okay, fine. I'm in the middle of fighting the urge to go downstairs again. You want to punish me for trying to sneak out? Fine. You can sleep in the bed. With me. We can even fool around—'cause we both know we've wanted to since the minute we walked into this suite. I can't sneak out if you're lying here beside me. I get it. But, that won't get me to admit that I like you. Because I don't. Like you. In that way."

Nothing she said hindered his approach.

"This isn't about you admitting you like me, or me liking you." He took one of her wrists and cuffed it to the headboard. "This is about you needing help and me helping you. And just so we're clear, Kamaria, you may be ready for no-strings sex, but I want something more."

He gently cuffed the other wrist. She tugged at her binds. One of her hands slid out easily. He gently bound her again, watching her the whole time. Everything south of her belly button throbbed. "What are you going to do to me?"

He tossed a strip of condoms on the nightstand. She felt her bottom lip begin to quiver. Whatever it was he wanted from her, it had gone way past "just liking" him. But she wasn't scared. She was…

Turned the hell on.

"Nothing." He threw back the comforter, kneeling between her legs. He lowered himself onto his elbows, stretching his back in the process. This didn't look like nothing to her. Every muscle in her shoulders went rigid. "…Much."

"I was only kidding about going to the casino."

"No, you weren't."

She watched him push himself back up. "Don't I get credit for not leaving the room?"

"No, you don't." He reached for her foot. For once, she couldn't read him.

"Well, then, now I'm really scared."

"The only thing you're scared of is the truth." He untied her sneaker, wiggled it off and chucked it across the room. He did the same with her other foot.

"You're not gonna get me to like you like this."

"I wasn't planning on it." His hands hovered over the button on her jeans. "I'm going to pull off your pants. Don't kick me."

She scooted away as best she could. "Hold on, I gave you the green light earlier and you pushed me away. Now, you wanna do it while you have me tied up?" She wasn't completely opposed to the idea, but what the hell? Maybe she should kick him.

"No, I'm putting you to bed." Even though her legs were now in prime kicking position, Jack held his ground. "Unless, you want to sleep in your jeans."

"Oh. But with handcuffs on?" She relaxed her knees. Their eyes met. As before, the connection between them flared. "Untie me. I can take them off myself."

He half quirked an eyebrow. "Yeah, but what fun would that be?"

Jack reached out again, making quick work of loosening her jeans. All the while, his eyes never left hers.

Her zipper opened with a flick. She lifted her hips and smiled, goading him. He swallowed. What was he doing? He had intended to tie her up and leave her there to teach her a lesson. But his newly discovered impulsive side urged him on to do more. So did her eyes.

The "old" him had always opted to do "the right thing." Tonight, it was time to go with the flow. "Are you sure?"

"Yes."

He shifted his weight to ease the ache straining the elastic limits of his boxer briefs. He stalked toward her on his hands and knees, like a panther hovering over his prey. His hand palmed her behind before slowly peeling away the form-fitting denim. What he found beneath made him swear.

She wasn't wearing any panties.

He, in turn, surprised her with the most intimate of kisses.

When Kamaria gasped, he grinned into her flesh. *That's right, sweetheart. You only thought you were in control.*

He kissed his way up to the tender flesh of her belly. "If at any time you want me to stop, say 'liverwurst.'"

"What?" Kamaria's eyes flew open.

"Our safe word."

"Liverwurst has got to be the least sexy thing to say during foreplay."

He hovered over her face, rubbing the very tip of his nose gently against hers. "That's the idea. My Nonna would make me eat liverwurst sandwiches every day after school. I hate the stuff. Mentioning it is the quickest way to pull me out of the mood."

"But when you think about it, deli meat looks kinda hot." She stroked the outline of his cock with her toes. He grabbed her foot, carefully extending the line of her leg until it rested on his shoulder. His nose nuzzled her inner thigh.

"I think you're hot."

Jack sank onto his elbows and knees. He buried his face into her sweetness, transporting him from memories of a cold cut nightmare—and Jesus, only this woman could make him laugh one second and have him hotter than hell in the next—to the impossible heat and beauty that was Kamaria Wilson. Each time her hips swayed or pitched forward, he was right there with her. Never relenting in his pursuit of her pleasure. He knew she was close when she started to pant.

"Jack. You... I..." He inserted his fingers into the mix to finally take her over the edge. Her entire body tensed, and then she convulsed, her body tightening. She made the sweetest, sexiest sounds he'd ever heard when she came.

He knew she had returned to earth when she gasped, "Liv...wurst."

He reached up to remove her hands from his cuffs. He had left them just loose enough for her to slip out with a gentle tug.

"Wait." The single word stopped him. "I want you to leave them on." Satisfaction warmed his belly. He could totally fall for this woman.

"Are you sure?"

"Yes." Everything about this was too right. There had to be a way to make this work between them past Sunday…

Still relishing his moment of glory, Jack rolled onto his back and closed his eyes. With her arms bound and body sprawled against the sheets like some exotic offering for his pleasure, she was the sexiest fucking thing he'd ever seen. He quickly slipped on a condom and slid deep into her heat.

"Faster. Please," she begged. He grinned as he felt her back arch.

"No." He continued to take his time despite feeling her clench and strain around his cock as he drove deep. "You're still in trouble, naughty girl."

"Please." She nuzzled against his chest, one leg massaging up along the side of his body. If he'd freed her hands, he knew they would've wrapped around him and held him close. He shook his head in response as he continued his leisurely pace. One agonizing stroke at a time.

"This is torture," she hissed. She raised her head so their chins touched.

"That's the idea, sweetheart." He wedged his hand between their bodies, reaching down to tease her clit between his fingers.

"What if…" He shifted his stroke and she gasped. A few labored breaths later, she continued. "What if I say the safe word?"

Dammit. He stopped and studied her face. Her eyes shone with mischief. He narrowed his eyes at her. "That's not gonna work this time."

He nuzzled the length of her neck as he picked up the

pace. Her sweet body arced again, tightening its seal around him. He responded with a flick of her right nipple. He had already figured out that one was the more sensitive of the two. She mewled her surprise. If she thought she could goad him into coming first, she had another thing coming. He had no intention of losing this round.

"Promise me." By now, he had her legs around his waist with every thrust hitting its mark. "Promise you'll still be in my arms when I wake up."

"I promise." And then her body shivered in surrender. Pulsing, clenching, dragging him over the edge with her in a shattering release.

A few seconds later, she smiled up at him. "I should be bad more often."

"Don't push your luck." He smiled against her skin. "I'm pretty sure you won't be sneaking off to go anywhere tonight."

Kamaria sighed. "Not. Funny…"

"Fine." He jiggled the chain between her cuffs with his fingers. "I won't do this again."

"The hell you won't." She slipped out of one of the cuffs and laced her fingers around his hand. He was happy to see her enjoying the intimacy between them. Finally.

He settled beside her. She snuggled up against him, a leg thrown across his hips, her head tucked beneath his chin. Her heart thudded against his. It was a while before her breathing slowed and her pulse settled.

"Tell me something I don't know about you." Her other hand found its way to his back. Score. He shifted and turned off the bedside lamp so she couldn't see his smile. His little gambler might not realize it, but she craved their intimacy as much as he did.

"I'm originally from Pennsylvania. My mother and my Nonna are still there. My baby sister is getting ready to graduate from college. Family means everything to me."

"What about your dad?"

That question made him hesitate. Would the truth make a difference to her? He decided to go for it. "He's dead. He ran up some gambling debts with the wrong people and…you know."

Her toes stroked his leg. "I'm sorry. And then someone like me pops into your life."

"Yeah. But you're different. You're actually *trying* to get better. It's one of the things I like about you." He reached over and stroked her face. "It's one of the things I *really* like about you. I know it's tough. And I know this doesn't make any sense, but I'd like to get to know you better, support you any way that I can."

There, he'd said it. The truth was, he was beginning to have all kinds of feelings about her. A slight catch interrupted the even rhythm of her breathing, but she was otherwise quiet.

"You don't have to say anything, Kamaria. I broke the 'it's over when someone gets caught up' rule. You win." Not that he was going to allow a few silly rules spoken in the heat of the moment to stop him from pursuing what he wanted. But, seriously, her silence was killing him. After a few seconds of deafening quiet, he had the sinking feeling that he'd overplayed his hand. He threw the pillow over his head.

"I…I like you too."

He swiped away the pillow. "What was that?"

"I said I like you too."

He cupped her face between his hands. "Are you serious?"

He felt her nod her head as he leaned in to kiss her. Her tongue met his in a desperate duel. This kiss was just as intense as the one they shared earlier. But this time, they were on the same page.

He butterfly kissed his way down her neck, finally landing on the hollow of her collarbone. She rewarded him with a moan when he traced the line leading to her shoulder with his tongue. She wrapped her legs around his waist. He sank his weight onto her torso just enough to hold her there.

She could go over-think why falling for him was a mistake later. "Seriously, you made me forget about all the temptation waiting for me outside that door. I feel like I'm using you."

Jack pulled her closer, tucked her on her side and draped an arm over her waist. "Then use me. I already told you, I'm not going anywhere."

"You're too nice for your own good. You've purposely made it too hard to not get attached to you."

"That was the idea, sweetheart. Now get some sleep."

Kamaria wiggled her butt against his still hard cock. "What about you? I'm down for round two."

"Tonight was all about you." He rubbed her hip. "Just don't tell Chastity."

"Not all of my business is Chastity's business."

Jack kissed her earlobe, causing her to shiver. "Good. Now go to sleep."

"Yes, Mr. Alderisi."

"Mm, I like the sound of that."

When Jack woke up, Kamaria was nestled against his side with her head on his chest. He grinned. Right where she was supposed to be.

He played with one of her locks that had fallen from her updo style. The expression on her face was the most serene he'd seen on her since they met. As much as he wanted to pursue this thing between them, he was beginning to see the toll that being in Las Vegas was taking on her.

Jack tightened his arm around her waist and gave it a quick squeeze. The best thing to do was make the most of this weekend, and then let her go home. But he didn't want to do the "right" thing anymore.

The truth was, he didn't want to let her go. He had to figure out a way to keep her close. She had mentioned something about living in Arizona. One state over. That was close enough, right?

She wriggled against him. "I really want you, Jack."

Jack fumbled for a condom on the nightstand. He pressed it into her hand. "Ride me."

Kamaria smiled in acknowledgment. "As you wish."

She made quick work of rolling the condom onto him. With the morning light streaming through the window, she looked the happiest he'd seen her since they met. He had to catch his breath as she lowered herself onto him. She pressed her hands into his chest, leveraging herself over him, joining them in one smooth glide. His breath shuddered out of him as she sucked the underside of his jaw.

She leaned forward and began sucking his earlobe. "I like the way you fill me."

She ground herself against him, circling her hips. Her figure eights around his cock felt better than any massage he'd ever had. He reached for her, but she was too quick. She grabbed his wrists and pinned them to his sides.

And then, she squeezed him. Like a damn clamp.

Jack never heard himself moan like that before. Could this woman be any more perfect?

"Yeah. I'm close too," she purred into his ear. Her vice-like hold on his cock eased. "But I'm not done with you yet."

He gave a short nod in response. Kamaria sank her full weight on him again. He cursed. The further he delved into her softness, the more his control slipped. He squeezed his eyes together. Then, she cried out as her core fluttered around him.

He gripped the sheets to keep from joining her. His control was slipping by the second. "Stop moving."

She stilled halfway up his cock. "I'm sorry I came so fast, Jack. That's never happened…"

He felt her thighs tremble as she readjusted herself.

"Please." His eyes flew open. Did he just whimper?

She looked as overwhelmed as he felt. The sunlight streaming from behind her made her post-coital glow turn golden. Her brown skin glistened with sweat, making her look like a bronze goddess. How could this woman be real?

He let go of the sheet to touch her. Oh yes, her warm, slick thigh was very real. He continued on to palm the soft flesh of her belly. Its slight give made her more real than any of the rail-thin showgirls on the Strip. He tweaked her nipple. Her breasts jiggled against the rise and fall of her chest as she struggled to regain her breath. Those were most definitely real.

"Jack, my leg. I can't…" She slipped back down his length.

"But I can." He rolled her over onto her back, sinking himself back into her depths. He shifted his angle. She clutched his forearms.

"There," she breathed. "Right there."

Them, together like this… God, it felt like home. He began moving. Slowly. Deeply. Tenderly. Taking care with each stroke to return to that same spot, to her "there."

His teeth gnashed together. Every muscle in his body tensed. If he relaxed, even a little, there would be nothing left to curb his release. He closed his eyes. He wanted to last for her. Hell, he wanted to last forever.

This moment felt like a turning point. The linchpin he needed to convince her that just this weekend would never be enough. Her mouth opened. Her bottom lip quivered. She pulled on his arms. He quickened his thrusts, complying with her unspoken request.

Her eyes rolled back. Then, dammit, she squeezed his cock and wailed as she came.

Her unexpected movement sent him over the edge. As the last of his control exploded, he could see it all with her—a wedding, babies, growing old together, everything. Those images—each one all too real. He cradled her head as he filled her with all his possibilities.

Their ragged breaths became one as he continued to plank himself over her. His biceps trembled from the exertion, but he was in no rush to break their physical connection. If only he had the power to stop time. There was no way he'd be satisfied with just this weekend now, but there was no way he would ask her to stay longer. He looked at the clock. Her speech was in little over an hour.

And just like that, good old responsible Jack was back. He rolled onto his side and broke the connection. "C'mon, it's getting late."

He stood, swept her into his arms, and carried Kamaria into the bathroom. He pushed the sliding door open, then turned on the water to its full spray strength.

Only then did he loosen his grip as he carefully placed her into the shower stall. He caressed her face. "Don't move."

He returned to the sink and rifled through the cabinet until he found a shower cap. He carefully covered all of her hair with it until the elastic band was secure around her hairline. "I saw how long it took you to twist and style your hair yesterday. I'll be damned if I get it wet again."

He guided her further into the shower. Then Jack unhooked the showerhead and proceeded to wash his woman. He had to chuckle to himself about those rules she had established. Hold back his emotions? Hell, he broke that rule on day one.

When he was finished, he twisted the knob to turn the water off. He turned his back just long enough to snatch a towel from the rack next to the shower. Then he got down on one knee and proceeded to carefully towel off her body. He paused to take extra special care of her breasts, lapping up any water droplets with his tongue. He felt her entire body shudder under his attentions, causing Jack to smile around her taut nipple. Her arms cradled his head. She didn't need him to shield her from temptation. She needed him to create a safe space for her to figure out how to deal with her demons on her own.

He swept her into his arms and carried her into the bedroom where he gently plopped her down on her bed.

He stood before her. His cock was ready for more. "I don't think I'll ever get enough of you."

Kamaria smiled saucily up at him. "You're not playing by the rules."

"I never was." He coaxed two more orgasms out of her before she reluctantly evoked their safe word again.

Kamaria played with a few strands of his hair between her fingers. In a quiet voice, she said, "Thank you."

"For the sex?" He stroked the length of her spine with his fingertips. His lips then followed in their wake. The delicious sensation made her shiver. "The pleasure was all mine."

"Well, thanks for that, too. But no, thanks for understanding. I might joke about it, but those poker tables downstairs were calling me like a siren's song. I'm too weak to fight it on my own sometimes." It was the first time she admitted so much out loud. Saying so felt like a cinder block had been lifted from her shoulders.

"That's my job." Jack crawled down the bed on his hands and knees to her feet. "That's why I'm here."

Kamaria took a quick glance at the clock on the nightstand. "Ugh, we really have to get going now."

"Mm-hm." He took her foot into his hands. It looked like

a toy cupped between his huge palms. Jack began kneading her sole with his fingers. Kamaria licked her lips. She could definitely get used to having this man around for the long haul. She quickly pushed that thought from her mind. Her life was such that she could pick up and live anywhere she wanted. Well, anywhere but here in Nevada. And Jack lived here.

Just enjoy the moment. She lowered herself from her elbows down to the bed. She had a tendency to over-think a good thing. She needed to break that habit. Starting now.

He proceeded to "help" her put on her shoes. Using his hands and tongue, he started at her feet, working his way up her legs and beyond. After he got her off, he pushed himself to his feet and retrieved her dress she had selected for the day. He lowered the dress carefully over her head. "That crazy agent of yours will have my head if I make you miss your speech."

"I'd much rather stay in bed with you." Kamaria bit her lip. "As a matter of fact, I'm thinking about extending my stay. I believe I owe you two more days together."

Jack stood up with his back to her. Each movement emphasized the definition in the musculature on his back. And then there was his ass… Chastity had been so right. He had a perfect ass.

"I don't think that's such a good idea." He flicked on his shirt. "C'mon. Let's get you downstairs."

Chapter Seven

The volume in the medium-sized ballroom increased the moment she and Jack stepped into the room. The chatter sounded like double the fifty or so people already seated. Since this luncheon was sponsored by an online book club that had recently featured her work, she knew the reason most likely had to do with both Jack's striking resemblance to the cover model on her book and the way they'd disappeared from the book signing the day before.

"I saw them running away from a screaming stampede…" She felt her cheeks warm at that wisp of loudly whispered gossip. She couldn't help feeling that more than one person in the crowd was speculating, with some accuracy, of how she and Jack had spent their evening. They must all think she was some kind of delusional celebrity who pumped her self-esteem by dragging around some boy toy.

Jack bent to whisper in her ear. "I need to stay here by the door." He tapped his security earpiece. "We're all on alert that some known troublemakers just entered the casino."

"Fine," she murmured. What was his deal? She admitted

her feelings, just like he wanted, and now *he* was pushing her away. She felt like such a fool. Yeah. It sucked. But she was a big girl. And she'd get through this day and then the rest of the conference and then she'd haul her ass far, far away from Vegas.

Focus. If only the room wasn't so cheery, so yellow. A few readers she recognized from the book signing, before everything went crazy, called out to her. She drifted over to greet them, hoping that the fear gripping her insides didn't show on her face. She was happy to see a pile of four or five books stacked at each place setting. She handed each of them a postcard with a free digital download code on them to add to their convention swag.

"Where's your cute friend from yesterday?" one of them asked.

So not the way she wanted to start the conversation. "He's, uh, working."

"Too bad. You two made such a cute couple. You need to hold onto him."

"Thanks." Even strangers had an easier time of accepting her relationship with Jack than she did. Kamaria lifted her chin and continued to swing her hips in what she hoped was a casual stroll around to the other tables.

"Girl, can you believe it? The casino still smells like cigarettes, wet dog, and a pre-teen girl's perfume drawer!" What the…?

She slowed her pace to catch more bits and pieces of conversation as she passed. She began to realize that all the whispering had less to do with her and Jack and more with some craziness that had gone down the previous night.

She smiled as she stopped to sign books for some readers who had been missed due to the mob at the book signing. But on the inside, she was a total mess. Her stomach felt like it was full of butterflies. A lump formed in her throat. She hated public speaking. She hated being the center of attention. Why in the world had she agreed to give this speech? Oh yeah, that's right. Chastity had talked her into it. Kamaria really needed to fire her.

Then she almost stumbled when she could hear bells ringing and people shouting from the casino. She felt her palms dampen. Her throat instantly went dry. That ever-present invisible vice tightened around her chest. She rounded her lips into an O and sucked in a gasp of air. She instantly went from a mild case of stage fright to feeling like she was kneeling before a chopping block.

Deep breath in. Slow breath out. Keep it together.

She pulled Toni, the president of the book club sponsoring the luncheon, by the arm. "Is it possible to close the door to block out the noise from the casino?"

"Oh yes, we'll be closing them soon. We're not scheduled to start for another fifteen minutes." Toni waved her arm toward the tables. "As you can see, only half the attendants have arrived."

Kamaria gave her a tight smile. "Of course. Thank you." She was doomed.

She looked around for Jack. He stood by the door, as promised, speaking to one of the more flirtatious convention attendees. The unnaturally pale woman was stroking his arm with her hand. Kamaria clenched her own hands into fists. Yes, there was no official commitment between the two of them. Yes, she had been the one who insisted on an emotion-free, no-strings-attached "sex only" relationship. But, this vampiric woman, in her almost-nothing outfit—really who wore a skirt *that* short—touching Jack? Kamaria didn't like it. And, she didn't like that it affected her so much. But she had no right to say anything. Jack would be free to do whomever he wanted once the convention ended tomorrow. It wasn't like the little skank would have a chance to bed Jack anytime soon anyway.

It was his job to be attached to her side until she checked out in the morning. In all honesty, the woman was doing little more than making a fool of herself.

That didn't stop Kamaria from wanting to scratch the woman's eyes out.

She turned her back to that non-drama and stepped onto the dais. Once seated, she took a deep breath as she forced herself to review her note cards. Her eyes began to glaze over the words she had scratched out about throwing caution to the wind and living your dreams. None of it felt true anymore.

One reader scrambled in as they were closing the ballroom doors and yelled, "I won five hundred dollars at poker!" Everybody cheered but Kamaria. Her hands became clammy again. The ever-present tight band around her chest made her breaths short. She stared off in the direction of the door. But beyond Jack. She needed to get in the casino while the tables were hot.

Toni tapped her on the shoulder. "Are you ready, hon?"

She jerked her head back into the present. She must have zoned out for more than a few minutes. She got that way sometimes when the urge to gamble was strong. She poured herself a glass of water.

The book club president's brow creased with worry. "Are you all right, Ms. Wilson?"

She swallowed a gulp of water. "I'm fine." She smiled at the woman, but on the inside her heart was racing. "I think I have a little stage fright. There sure are a lot of people here."

Toni gave her shoulder a squeeze. "You'll be fine. If it helps, just remember that most of the men in attendance are in their underwear. Literally." The woman giggled at her own joke. Kamaria forced a laugh. Little did Toni know that hard pecs and sock-enhanced boxer briefs weren't the only things she craved right now. She wanted Jack by her side.

"Okay, sugar. You're up." The book club president went

up to the podium to call the room to order. She didn't hear any of the woman's remarks nor her introduction. The muffled cheers coming from the casino kept her enraptured. Luckily, Chastity was right beside Kamaria to nudge her out of her daze.

"Hey, Mari. You don't look so good."

Even Jack, who had pried his eyes away from his female admirer, was now looking at her with concern in his eyes. How sweet of him to start acting like he cared again. Kamaria tossed her note cards to the side. She pushed herself to her feet. "I'm fine."

She stood behind the microphone for a moment. She cleared her throat. "Sorry, I'm not much of a public speaker. For those of you who follow me on social media, you know that I do my best talking with a keyboard."

That quip generated a few laughs. Kamaria felt some of the tension in her neck loosen. "I wanted to speak to you today about going out on a limb to live your dreams and all that stuff…"

Her eyes went back to the doorway again. Jack was still there but he was no longer looking in her direction, but at the floor. He had his finger to his ear, like he was blocking out her voice. His head whipped toward the hallway. Then, he ran out. Her heart plummeted. Using a man as her security blanket was the stupidest thing ever. She was on her own now.

She swallowed. She returned her attention to her audience. Everything she planned to say evaporated from her mind. She looked over to Chastity, who was on the verge of popping up to rescue her. She held up her hand. "No, Chastity. I don't need you to save me anymore. I got this."

She adjusted the microphone, as much out of nervousness as the need to adjust to her short stature. "The truth is…I shouldn't be here. In Las Vegas, I mean. I have a gambling problem. My grandmother raised me on her own after my parents died. There were days when there wasn't enough money for food. I started playing poker in high school as a way to keep my grandma's belly full and her medicine cabinet stocked. When you grow up like that and you can make a thousand dollars in a few rounds of cards, there's no such thing as winning enough. I always needed 'just one more' hand.

"My 'just one more time' obsession caused my grandma to die alone. When the hospital called to tell me that Grandma was dying and asking for me, I was here in Vegas playing 'one more hand' of poker. That was three years ago. I hadn't played again until yesterday.

"My grandma loved reading romance novels. I started writing my own books to honor her in light of the horrible thing I had done. For some strange reason, you wonderful people chose to read those books, over and over again. I don't deserve the attention and accolades you as readers have bestowed upon me.

"So, today I stand before you as the recently crowned bestselling author that you all made me. But the plain old truth is my name is Kamaria Wilson…and I'm a gambling addict. Standing here with that casino floor mere footsteps away is killing me, you guys. But it was important to me to thank you, the readers, for supporting me like you have. I love you all. Thank you."

To her amazement, everyone stood and applauded. A sense of acceptance filled the room and embraced her. She had revealed her shameful secret and no one seemed to think she was some horrible person. As a matter of fact, they seemed to regard her as Jack had all weekend—with admiration.

This realization caused all the tension to leave her body. The love she received in return for her public admission? That sent her soaring into the clouds. The pull of the casino was no more. She was free, at least for today. She had to tell Jack. He might not "want" her or to take their relationship further, but he'd been an integral part in helping her find her strength and he deserved her thanks.

Kamaria left the dais, then ran out of the ballroom. She stood in the middle of the hallway looking every which way for Jack. She remembered he had mentioned something about a possible problem in the casino. Maybe he had gone there. She jogged down the stairs leading into the casino without any thought. Just past the entrance to the poker pit, she could see a number of the security staff, Jack included, wrestling a man to the ground. Curiosity got the better of her as she inched closer to the tussle. Too close, actually. A wild arm flew out of the melee, sending her flailing backward. She stumbled a few steps until she walked into an unoccupied chair and plopped down on it heavily.

The dealer at the table took her sitting there as a sign that she wanted to play. He held out his hand to take her bet. "Welcome to the table, little lady! How much are you playing for today?" She held her hands over the table, almost like she was covering a hand of cards. "No, wait…"

She looked up and saw a disheveled Jack standing behind the dealer. His chest heaved up and down like he was out of breath. But his eyes shone with utter disappointment.

Jack came around the table. He hoisted her up by the arm. "I leave you alone one time… Did you really just walk out on your speech to come in here?"

"Yes, I did. I…"

"Kamaria Wilson, I'm going to have to ask you to leave the premises. Immediately…"

A single tear streamed out of the corner of her eye. Now she understood why Jack dismissed her suggestion about spending a few more days together. It could never work out between them. Not as long as he made his home here in Las Vegas. He would always see her as an addict who needed a babysitter.

She swiped the tear away with the back of her hand. "You're right, Jack. I don't belong here."

Yanking her arm free of his grasp, she dashed out of the casino toward the elevator bank. She smashed the button repeatedly until the door opened. Her heart hurt, not because of Jack's knee-jerk reaction to what he saw, but because she had no say in how "what could have been" ended. Just like every other major change in her life. The end of her life as a professional gambler. Leaving Las Vegas in defeat instead of victory. Allowing herself to fall for Jack, a man she could never have, had been a bad bet.

She entered the elevator that would take her back to her suite with her head hung low. Her legs trembled. She slid down until she was sitting on the elevator floor. She cradled her head between her arms and opened her mouth to sob. But nothing came out.

Now that the pull of the casino was gone, she felt completely empty.

Chapter Eight

A few weeks later, Jack was back doing "just one more favor" for Ben, filling in for one of the guys who had called in sick. They had just caught some guy counting cards. Jack was in the process of throwing the scumbag into a metal folding chair in the security office.

Ben had to grab Jack by the shoulders to haul him off the guy. "Whoa there, Alderisi. What bug crawled up your ass?"

Jack yanked his shoulder out of Ben's grasp. He shot both Ben and the perp an evil eye. "He lied to me," he ground out between clenched teeth. "I don't like it when they lie."

Ben was now standing between the two men, with one hand on each man to keep them apart.

"You, asshole. In the chair. Now." Ben pushed the perp down into the chair and handcuffed his hands behind his back. Then he turned toward Jack. "You. Outside."

Once they were in the hallway, Ben read Jack the riot act. "What is your deal? You've been a grumpy bastard for weeks now."

"I'm fine."

"No, you're not. Not since that romance convention ended. Have you called her yet?"

"Who?"

Ben fumbled inside his desk drawer and produced a business card. He handed it to Jack. "You know who."

It was Chastity Rollin's card. Kamaria's agent. "It didn't work out between us. Leave it alone, Ben."

"If you don't call, I will."

"Fine." He had never gotten Kamaria's phone number. Sending her an email through her author website felt too creepy. Chastity had all but thrown them together. Maybe she would help him find her. He grabbed his suit jacket and headed for the door. "You look like you can handle it without me."

Ben called out after him, "Yeah. Now get your shit together."

Jack stomped down the hallway toward the employee parking area. He slammed the door behind him. Once he was in his truck, he loosened his tie. He was done with these part-time weekend security gigs anyway. He was at a point of turning away home renovation jobs during the week.

He pulled his cell phone out of the inner lining pocket of his jacket. He didn't want to think about Kamaria anymore. Or her big brown eyes. Or her seductive smile. Or how, despite his resemblance to the hero on her book, he failed to be the hero she needed him to be in real life. He wanted to hold her. Use his hands and his mouth to show her how sorry he was. He hadn't been able to think about anything else since she left town. And, damn it, he missed her.

His cell phone vibrated in his hand. It was his sister Sofia. He swiped the screen to answer it.

"What?" he barked into the phone.

"Hello to you too, big brother." Sofia sounded way too cheery.

He took a deep breath. "What can I do for you?"

"I just wanted to remind you that my graduation is coming up in a few weeks. Since you handled most of my tuition, I wanted to give you first dibs on tickets. But it sounds like you'd rather not be bothered. I'll let you go."

"Wait. My bad. You just caught me at a bad time. Your graduation is important." Jack forced his voice to soften. "Of course I'll be there."

"What's her name? Should I put you down for two tickets?"

"What makes you think there's a 'her'?"

"It's me, Jack."

"Okay, fine. She's one of those romance authors…"

"Which one?"

"Her name is Kamaria…"

"Oh my God, you met Kamaria Wilson? Why didn't you tell me?" Sofia made a high-pitched "ee" sound. Jack had to hold the device away from his ear until she finished.

"Yeah, her."

"Why'd you say 'her' like you're PMSing?"

"Sofia," Jack warned.

"Oh my God, you're sprung, aren't you? This is so freaking cool. My brother is in love with Kamaria Wilson. You totally have to bring her to my graduation. I'm telling Mama."

"Sofia!"

"I gotta go anyway. Whatever you did to screw it up with her, fix it. I can't wait to meet my future sister-in-law. Bye!"

Jack threw his phone onto the passenger side seat. Great. Knowing Sofia, she and their mother would have a wedding all planned and booked by the time he saw them at graduation. He started the ignition and pulled out of the parking space. Traffic exiting the property onto the Strip was backed up. It looked like it wouldn't be moving anytime soon. Chastity's business card was still sitting on his lap.

He imagined Sofia's pout if he showed up at her graduation without Kamaria on his arm. So he had to invite her, right?

Besides, he could see Kamaria becoming fast friends with his sister. She would adore his tough-as-nails mother. Mama didn't let anyone push her around anymore, either. And then his grandmother... He could see Nonna giving Kamaria the secret family cannoli recipe as soon as she laid eyes on her.

He snatched up his phone. He was such a sucker. His little sister had him wrapped around her finger, even from three thousand miles away. Not that he could really blame Sofia, it was Kamaria that had him tied in knots. Yes, he'd been a bastard lately, but only because he'd been hurting for any excuse to go after her. "Christ, fine. I'll call."

He didn't need to look at the card. This wasn't his first time dialing the number on it. But, this was the first time he stayed on the line long enough for someone to answer.

"Tough Ta-Tas Literary Management."

Jack took a deep breath. "Chastity, it's Jack Alderisi."

"You say that like I should know who you are." From the tone of her voice, she knew exactly who he was. And she didn't sound too happy to hear from him. He steeled himself for an uphill battle.

"The security guy you hired," he replied slowly. "From Vegas."

Silence.

"Where is she?" Jack winced as he blurted out the question. He sounded desperate, even to himself.

"Oh, Mr. Alderisi. It's been so long I figured you weren't ever going to call."

Her snarky jab hit him in the chest. "I deserve that."

"Yes, you do. I was disappointed with how you handled my client at the end of that weekend. My gut told me you were the man for the job. I've never been wrong before... Too bad. 'Cause you have a really nice butt. Did Mari ever tell you that she has a thing for nice butts?"

Jack could tell that Chastity was smiling now. He released the breath he had been holding. "I know I fucked up. I have no idea how to fix it. I need your help."

"I thought you'd never ask." He could hear her ruffling through some papers on the other end. "Kamaria mentioned that you do home renovations. Is that true?"

"Yes, ma'am. But what does that have to do with Kamaria?"

"She's at my family's property in Arizona. The place could use some work. It's several hours from Vegas by car. I doubt she'll open the door for you if you're only there to say you're sorry. But she might if you tell her you're there to do an estimate on the warped floor for me."

"You don't have to hire me for a job. If it'll help me make things right with Kamaria, I'll do the work for free."

"Nice ass and you do freebies? Kamaria was right. You are the perfect man. Please don't mess this up with her again."

The traffic light changed. The cars in front of him started moving, giving Jack just enough space to turn off onto a less crowded side street.

"I won't," he promised. "Just text me the address. I'm on my way."

Kamaria stared off at the red rock formations in the distance. Being in Sedona usually gave her the peace of mind she needed to tackle huge chunks of writing. But not this time. Whenever she sat down at her laptop, all she could think about was Jack.

She pushed away from her desk, causing her chair to roll backward. Dammit. She didn't know why she was so hung up on this guy. There were so many reasons why nothing long term could ever happen between them. But the fact that the last time she saw him, he had automatically assumed the worst of her… She wondered how something that should've been insignificant had the power to devastate her so much.

What happened in Vegas was supposed to stay in Vegas.

She looked out the window again. She saw a pickup truck pull into the driveway. It said *Alderisi Home Renovations* on the side. It couldn't be… Kamaria snatched up her phone and called Chastity.

"Tough Ta-Tas Literary Management."

"Chastity, tell me why Jack's truck is parked in front of the house."

"Oh yeah, I forgot to tell you. I have someone coming out to do an estimate for some renovations."

Kamaria pinched the bridge of her nose. "Chastity, you don't forget anything. And this isn't a random someone outside."

"I can't help it if the fix-it guy happens to be cute." Kamaria watched Jack jump out of his truck and look around the property. "I have it on good authority that he has a great ass."

Kamaria tightened the sash on her robe. She glanced in the mirror. Her cleavage still peeked out. Her tousled locks framed her face. Today would be the day that she looked like a disheveled sex goddess. God, would he think that she'd planned to greet him in only a silk robe? Helloo, desperate much? She could run upstairs. Maybe hide. Change into some clothes. "Please tell me that you hired a look-alike male prostitute to put Jack's business logo on a truck and drive all the way out here."

Chastity sighed. "I can't, because I did no such thing. I didn't hire anybody to drive anywhere. He called me."

She could hear his boots crunch up the gravel walkway.

When he reached the rickety step outside of the screen door, it shook the whole house. He tapped the knocker against the door.

"He's here. I can't believe he's here. Chastity, I'm gonna get you for this."

"How about getting me a decent maid of honor dress for the wedding? Have fun, Mari. You're getting a second chance. Don't mess this one up, hon."

The dial tone rang in her ear. Who was thinking about wedding bells when she and Jack couldn't even figure out the first date?

A second heavy knock on the door made her jump. She flew down the staircase to the ground floor and yanked open the door. She quickly folded her arms across her chest.

"Kamaria." Jack breathed her name through the screen door.

"What are you doing here, Jack?" Even though he still stood on the lower step, his chin cleared the top of her head by a few inches. She felt her nipples pebble beneath her arms at the sound of his voice. She squeezed herself tighter. No, she wouldn't cave that easily. He was the one who had been in the wrong.

"Can I come in?"

She felt her pulse quicken. The tortured look in his eyes made her want to reach out to him. No. She needed to stand her ground. "That depends. Chastity said she wants you to look over the house for a renovation estimate. So, did you come all this way for Chastity…or are you here for me?"

"I came for you." Jack shifted the tool box under his arm. "But she wasn't kidding when she said this house needed some work. I'm glad Chastity asked me to come out to take a look."

"Come out to take a look?" Kamaria stepped aside and pushed the screen door open. "You make it sound like you were around the corner instead of a four-hour drive away."

"It was no biggie. The landscape on the way was almost as beautiful as you."

He came for me. She would've swooned if she wasn't supposed to be mad at him. If this is what those grand gesture moments in romance novels actually felt like, she had been totally writing them wrong. "Ha! Cute. Just keep the noise down while you do whatever you need to do. I have a book to finish."

"No problem." The normal gleam in his eyes looked flat. But his expression told her nothing. Now, of all times, *now* he was going to master a poker face.

"Jack, seriously, why are you here?"

"I told you. I'm. Here. For. *You.*"

"Chastity said you called her. What about all that talk about keeping her out of our business?"

Jack paused. "We didn't part on the best of terms. And I never got your phone number so I could contact you directly."

"All of my contact information is in the hotel database. Why didn't you swipe it from there?"

"Because that…" Jack pulled open the screen door. He stepped forward to brush a stray lock from her face. "…Is considered stalking."

"And showing up like this isn't?"

"I was invited."

"Not by me."

"It's not your house."

Kamaria scrunched up her face. "That's not entirely correct. What did Chastity tell you?"

"Nothing, except the address and that this was her family's property. Look, I know I hurt you. I assumed the worst without gathering the facts. I apologize for that. Chastity told me what happened. How you had that breakthrough during your speech. I hate that I missed it." Jack paused to run his hand through his hair. Kamaria wished he hadn't done that. The gesture made her want to drag him upstairs into her bed. "She told me how you came into the casino to tell me about it, not to play."

She nodded her head.

"All I wanted to say was that I'm proud of you. And that I'm sorry." Jack picked up his gear. "I'll get to looking the place over now. We can keep it strictly professional this time. I won't bother you again."

"Wait." She grabbed Jack by the arm. "Why did you brush me off when I said I was ready to take us past that weekend?"

Jack stared at her hand. She detected a ghost of a smile curving his lips. "I didn't mean it that way. Of course I wanted to keep seeing you, but *away* from Las Vegas."

"So…" She returned his smile. This was starting to feel like a middle school "you hang up first" conversation.

"Don't you have a book to finish, Kamaria?"

"Don't you have a major renovation to plan? Look, thanks. Your apology. I appreciate that. So what now?"

"If you think you're ready, I'd love to have something more with you. I told you I'm not a fling kind of guy. I'm all in or nothing. But, I care enough to not put you in a situation that's not good for you. It's not like I can ask you to come back to Vegas with me."

"And I can't ask you to stay here with me in the boonies. You have a business to run."

"A business that sometimes requires working on projects out of town," he reminded her. Jack tapped his boot upon the warped wooden floor in the living room. He looked back to inspect the creaky screened porch he had just walked through.

"Chastity wasn't kidding about these floors. How old is this house?"

"About a hundred years old. Why?"

"That means it definitely needs some work done

somewhere. With a house this old, it might take a few weeks." He leaned forward so they were eye to eye. "Do you think that would be long enough for us to figure something out?"

"I can't ask you to stay here and work on my house for free."

"Your house? Chastity said that this house belonged to her family."

"I was on a winning streak the year before my grandma passed. She said it was her dream to die surrounded by the beauty of the desert. So, Chastity and I bought this for her. Technically, it's *our* house."

"You have a pretty generous agent."

"She's my agent *and* my cousin. She's also a nosy busybody."

"…Who thinks I have a great ass. That's payment enough for any renovations."

"Maybe. But I say you still send her an invoice with a few zeros added. Let her freak out a bit before we tell her it isn't real." Kamaria pulled Jack back into the house and shut the front door. She took a handful of his delicious ass and squeezed. "As long as she continues to maintain her 'look but don't touch' policy on this ass, then she doesn't have to pay."

"Speaking of paying, I believe this belongs to you." Jack tossed her an odd colored coin. She snatched it out of the air and looked it over. It was her lucky poker chip. The one she would squeeze when the desire to play again came on too strong. Her anchor during the toughest days. The one he had taken from her that first day in the casino.

"You kept it?"

He shrugged. "You said it was special. And since I was the one who caved first, I thought you deserved it."

"You caved first on what?"

"Our bet. Remember, your rule about no emotions, blah blah blah?"

"Oh that." She looked up at him and stood on her tiptoes so she could wrap her arms around his neck. Man, he was gorgeous. She'd hit the jackpot this time. "You know I was full of it, right? I knew I liked you even then."

"Of course. But I knew if I raised the stakes, then we would both win." He kissed her on the nose.

"So what did we win?"

"Forever, if we play our cards right."

"I'll bet on that." She pulled him closer and kissed him.

Acknowledgments

Diallo, Saran and Daddy–thank you for keeping me sane while I finished this story.

Mommy and Miz Alice–thank you for tolerating my reclusive writer ways...and moods (smile).

Vanessa–thank you for your input and patience...on all 7 rounds.

A special shout out to all my RSJ peeps, my Voices at VONA peeps, my Depressed Elephant crew and my Popular Fiction Auteurs peeps–I don't think you all realize how much I love, appreciate, and miss you guys.

About the Author

Kaia Danielle writes romance, women's fiction and a graphic novel that is resisting the revision process. She tweets about being a Jersey Girl in South Georgia and popular culture in general on her @kaiawrites handle. She is an alum of the VONA writing workshop. Her website is www.kaiawrites.com

About the Author

www.ingramcontent.com/pod-product-compliance
Lightning Source LLC
Chambersburg PA
CBHW031130210626
46816CB00015B/1378